Dawn French Bo
Lamp
✢
other short stories

by

Lisbeth Foye

Copyright © 2015 by Lisbeth Foye

Also by Lisbeth Foye

The Biggest Lie
Truth Unscrewed

Betsy Moonfish Cover Design

All rights reserved. Without limiting the rights under copyright observed above, no part of this publication may be reproduced, stored in or introduced into a retrieval system, or transmitted in any form or by any means without the prior written consent of the copyright owner.

This is a work of fiction. Names, characters, businesses, places, events and incidents are either the products of the author's imagination or used in a fictitious manner. Any resemblance to actual persons, living or dead, or actual events is purely coincidental.

Contents

1. Together Again   3
It's all about the choices we make - in this life, and the next

2. History Of A Stick   20
The ongoing repercussions of a murder, in 1899

3. Dawn French Bought My Lava Lamp   37
A solution to everything ... or, perhaps not

4. Peculiar Ways   54
The tale of a man who followed the road of fate

5. The Whistleblower   72
A welcome comeuppance

6. The Story Of Thomas Cotter   93
They all assumed he lived a quiet life ...

7. Luca   141
A brief encounter for the twenty-first century

1. Together Again

My name does not give you a good indication of my age. My name probably creates a picture for you, of an elderly lady with, perhaps, a cluster of grandchildren tottering around.

But no, I don't even have any children. Not yet.

But once tomorrow comes, everyone will expect it of me; the patter of tiny feet is what the conversations will be, words whispered quietly as they sip their sherry from a small sensually shaped glass.

Who coined that phrase anyway, *the patter of tiny feet?* It's actually quite a nice way of saying it, despite it being an overused cliché.

I don't like clichés.

I, Nora Vine am nearly twenty-five years old and tomorrow, my life will change; I am to marry Bigsy.

****

I met Mark Biggs six years ago, at a barn dance would you believe, not really my thing, barn dances, I only went to please my mum. Her old pen pal was over from France, she liked line-dancing and all that cowboy stuff, so we all traipsed along: mum, dad, Yvette the pen pal, with husband *Sacha Distel* – that wasn't his real name, that was what my mum called him – then there was me and my brother Sid.

Me and Sid both expected a night of dullness but we really surprised ourselves, we had a blast of a time. Sid made friends with a young lad called Mark Biggs; and that's how it all began.

A couple of years ago Sid left us to go on a backpacking trip through South East Asia, he was only supposed to be gone for a couple of months but he met some Aussies and ended up in Melbourne, Australia. He's now working in a trendy restaurant and living with his Australian girlfriend. He won't be back in a hurry, and I can't say I blame him, I know where I'd rather be right now.

Sid won't be at my wedding tomorrow, he's skint with no money for the air fare.

Maybe if he was here, it would be different.

I wanted to delay the wedding just to give us, and Sid, a chance to save a bit of money so that we could get him back home for it. I love my brother, he's my twin, we started out together in mum's womb and, by rights, he should be here at my wedding.

This is a wedding on a budget. I bought everything online; my dress, bridesmaid's dress, all the bits to go with them like tiara and veil – all that stuff, I got everything for less than a hundred quid.

All brand new and shipped from China.

Bigsy's a good man, he's kind, thoughtful, loyal, and he works long hard hours at the supermarket, it's one of those superstores open twenty-four hours a day, which means shift work. Bigsy plans to be assistant manager within a couple of years.

The problem is, I feel no passion. My soul doesn't soar and spin around the moon, laughing with the joy at the prospect of spending my life with him.

His jokes don't make me laugh, yet I care for him so dearly.

And then I feel guilty because I lack the ability to love him as much as he deserves to be loved, I can't give him the devotion he deserves. My best friend Mandy, now, she would be perfect for him, even their names together sound better: Mark & Mandy, much better than Mark & Nora don't you think?

A wedding on a budget; the flowers have been done by my aunt Ada, she did a flower-arranging course at the local college; every Thursday evening for six weeks. She only completed the course so that she could do my flowers, she has even grown the blooms herself, bless her. She's hoping to get more work on the back of my wedding, I hope she does because then, at least, something good will have come out of the day.

My mum has made the cake and arranged the food for the finger buffet in the village hall.

Mandy is my chief, and only, bridesmaid.

The Big Day

The sun is shining.

I should be happy but I'm petrified.

It's 9 a.m. on my wedding day and I want to go back to sleep, I wish it was yesterday. I want every day to be yesterday.

In less than four hours I have an appointment at a church.

Mandy's still asleep, she slept over last night. I can hear mum and dad in the kitchen downstairs getting a pot of tea on the go.

Sid found, and then followed, his dream, he didn't get sucked into a life of pleasing others. I want to wake up and find my dream, but it's alluded me so far and so, I walk the road which they've laid out for me.

I make a noise and Mandy stirs.

'What are you doing?' she asks in a gravelly voice, the one people have when they've just woken up.

'I need a double espresso,' I reply as I tug and zip up my tight jeans.

'Ada will be here shortly to do your hair and make-up, don't be too long.' Mandy sits up in bed and looks around the room like she has never seen it before.

Last year my aunt Ada started a hairdressing and beauty course at the local college, she'd only completed two terms before giving up, 'don't worry,' she said, 'I've learned enough to make you look like a princess on your special day.' That worried me greatly.

All that standing played havoc with her bunions, she said. So she gave up. She didn't lose out though, she'd got herself one of those 24+ loans which paid for it and, she doesn't have to pay it back until she hits a high salary, which, of course, will never happen. She has signed up to do the pottery course which starts next term. That's our future birthday presents sorted then.

My heart is thudding in my chest, I feel acid burning my throat as I check my handbag to make sure I have everything, purse, phone – switched off - I need to get out of the house before it's too late. I finalised my decision at 3am this morning.

I bend and kiss the top of Mandy's head before I leave, I love her so dearly, the love I feel for my friend is nearly as strong as my love for Sid. Having Mandy marry my brother would have been the best thing ever, but I know it could never be. Sid's too adventurous and loves the rush of adrenalin too much. Mandy gives the impression of staidness and security, she makes you feel that she can solve all your problems, she will take care of it and the pain will go away.

She's the earth's core and Sid is the sky.

But Mark, on the other hand, would be a perfect match. Mandy sees the good in others and brings out the best in them; she would be the tree for his nest.

That's why I'm trusting her with the letter. Because *a)* I'm a weak coward and *b)* she will take care of the situation, she will understand and everything will come full circle to find its best resting place. And now I must go before it is too late to stop the avalanche.

<u>10:15 a.m.</u>

I've had too much coffee it's made my mouth dry and my stomach curdle – although that could be the guilt and the nerves I suppose. I need to hang out somewhere for a while, until the deadline has passed and Mandy has found my letter and the wedding has been cancelled. I need to find somewhere they won't think of looking for me in our small town, the coffee shops are the first place they'll send the troops.

Right now I detest myself so much I cannot bear to be in my own company.

I'm not sure why I came here, to the bus station, but it's an ideal place to kick about for a couple of hours, I've got some water, a newspaper and I can sit and watch people coming and going.

I wonder if Mandy has gone to take her dress out of the garment cover yet? As soon as she pulls down the zip she'll find the letter. I'm tempted to switch my phone on to see if she's messaged me, but I'm too afraid to see the consequences of what I've done.

An hour later

'This must be her…she's forgotten her key!' Nora's father shouted to the small gathering in the kitchen as he went to answer the knock on the front door.

'Well thank goodness for that, she's cutting it mighty short,' aunt Ada muttered before allowing a big huff of air to tremble through her lips.

'She just needed some space…' Mandy offered her viewpoint as she sat at the kitchen table in her dressing gown with a head full of oversized Velcro rollers.

'Mr Vine?' the police officer asked in a hushed voice.

'Yes…' he replied cautiously looking from the female officer to the man who had spoken.

'May we come in?' The young police officer asked, he'd already stood back to allow the female officer to enter the house first.

Nora's dad stood aside to let them both in, he gripped the door handle to steady himself. 'Is it Nora?' His own words didn't make much sense to him.

The police officers didn't respond to his question.

'Is your wife at home?' the female officer asked.

Mrs Juliet Brown's Statement
as told to the police officers at the scene

'I may be nearly seventy years of age but I'm still very nimble, I do yoga each day…' Mrs Brown inhaled, held her breath, exhaled slowly. 'But it all happened so quickly…'

'If you could just tell us the sequence of events, as you

remember them,' the police officer asked kindly and smiled softly.

'Yes, yes of course,' Mrs Brown's hands were shaking. 'I was making my way to Bay 15 for the bus. As I walked, I was rummaging in my bag which was hanging from my shoulder, it all happened so quickly...' She stopped mid-sentence to do her breathing exercise again to gain composure. 'I felt someone knock into me from the side and then they grabbed my bag, they tried pulling it away from me but I held onto it for as long as I could, I must have shouted and screamed and then they hit me and I fell to the ground.' Mrs Brown gently rubbed the side of her head where the fist had thumped hard into her skull, knocking her off-balance.

'Did you get a good look at him? The man who assaulted you?'

'Oh, it wasn't a man,' Mrs Brown said with a touch of incredulity, 'it was a young woman.'

'Sorry, my mistake...Then what happened?'

'The robber ran off with my bag, that's when another young woman came from out of nowhere, she yelled at the robber to stop – which of course they're not going to do, are they?'

The police officer handed a tissue to Mrs Brown who was trying to hold back the tears.

'The other young woman – the one who came to help me – well she dropped her own handbag on the ground next to me, telling me to look after it, then she ran hell for leather, after the robber. By now a crowd had gathered around me, one gentleman helped me up. And then I saw the woman - who I now know to be Nora – still chasing the robber, she ran, zig-zagging around the buses and across the concourse, then...' Mrs Brown's voice cracked and she sobbed, 'the coach came round the corner and ran straight into her, it threw her into the air…'

'It's alright, take your time.' The woman officer touched her arm.

'I saw the robber look back, she'd seen what happened but *still* she ran off, leaving Nora on the ground, in a heap…dead.'

<u>The time of day is unimportant</u>

Everything around me is calm, I feel so light. I had no idea how heavy and draining gravity was, how it pulls the body down with an unescapable weight, a heaviness which we live with every day of our lives, gravity is dreadful. I realise just how weary it made me feel.

What I feel now is love: pure, complete love which is more intense and tangible than anything I've ever experienced before, the light is different too, it's alive with energy, an energy which thrives on nothing but goodness.

I felt the thud on my body when the bus hit me but, before I had hit the ground a jolt shook me and I separated, well it must be my soul I think, it, *I* jumped out of my body. I looked down and in a strange, disconnected way, as my body flew through the air and landed in a heap, I felt no emotion for the empty shell lying there on the ground. I looked very odd.

I stood amongst the crowd looking down on me, their words were lost to sound but I knew what they were saying. The majority felt it was a tragedy *they* had to bear, seeing what happened to me somehow ruined their day. Only a couple of people emitted empathy which didn't reverberate back to themselves.

Then I turned and saw Original Sid coming towards me.

I can't tell you how thrilled I was to see him; he died twelve years ago and still, every Christmas, we laid a place at the table for him.

We called him Original Sid because he was already there when my brother came along. He was our uncle and he was so much fun. He made us bungee ropes and hung them from an old oak tree in the park which we swung and sprang around on.

He made a raft which didn't make it across the pond, we had to go home covered in green slime, my mum gave him a right telling off and told him he should grow up. Anyway, that was Original Sid and then, there he was, coming towards me, smiling and all aglow with all this intense love flying around, like fireflies on a full moon.

We communicate, not by speech as such, we both seem to say odd words here and there but it's a *knowing,* a connection of minds which is so absolutely natural.

He reminds me of the wedding, my family. I don't feel sorrow; sadness is an emotion for the living, I know that everything has a reason and nothing is so bad that it destroys you but, I'm also aware that we need to try and console those we love, send peace to envelop those we left behind, and give them strength. It is my duty to go and ease the chaos I have left behind.

****

Me and Original Sid are in the kitchen, everyone is crying. I know that the letter is still in the dress, Mandy hasn't yet found it. I also know that its content would only cause them more pain. I can't allow anyone but Mandy to find that letter.

I stand amongst my family shouting, telling them I still live – not in the same way but I am with them, still. My energy falls on deaf ears.

Original Sid knows better, he lets me know that he's been with us so many times and we always ignored him - that amuses me and I laugh, but it doesn't come out like a laugh.

And yet, sometimes he did get through, but we didn't realise it was him; we thought it was our own gut feelings sending us down one way or up another.

I let Original Sid know that we have to get Mandy upstairs so that she can find the letter, and as I think this, I know that there's nothing to worry about, we'll get through to her; that is a certainty.

It's working, I think our love and compassion is filtering through, I just heard my mum say that she can feel me in the room, she feels comforted she says, and then, she said:

'She'll be safe, she'll be with Original Sid, he'll look after her now.'

That thought from her shows me we've connected, well it fills me with a soaring joy that explodes in that little back kitchen, I feel aunt Ada shudder as that room rolls with the energy, the hairs on her arms and neck tingle – she feels us too. But they are all unaware of our presence, if only they would re-align their mind, just a little bit, they would feel the click of our connection.

Bigsy is stood by the worktop, he doesn't speak, the tears flow though, he sobs at my mum's words and then, I feel a deep love for him, a love I never felt when I was in the body. I want to protect him and have him know joy beyond words, he deserves to have so much more.

And then I notice someone else in the kitchen, my brother Sid, for the first time since my passing I feel a tad confused.

Original Sid fills me in, in one flash I know that Bigsy saved every penny he had. When he told me, a couple of months ago, that his beloved motorbike was knackered and that he'd taken it to the scrapyard, that hadn't actually been true. He'd sold his bike and with the proceeds from that, and selling other odd bits he had, he'd raised and saved enough money to buy a ticket for Sid to come home.

Sid was to be his best man, it was to be a surprise for me, and everyone else.

I bet his speech would have been a cracker.

Me and Original Sid hover close to Mandy, it doesn't take long. Perhaps grief allows the wavelengths to be more in tune to pick up the sensitivity of the spirit world? Mandy goes upstairs and straight to her dress hung on the side of the wardrobe. She lowers the zip and the letter falls out.

The Letter

My Mandy

You know how much I love and appreciate you, don't you? You're the best friend anyone could ever have, and you are *my* best friend. By the time you've finished reading this letter you may hate me, I won't blame you, but I also know that once it all calms down, that your hate will have disappeared, and that's the best I can hope for.

There's no way of saying this easily, so here goes:

Mandy, I don't love Bigsy as a wife should love her husband. I can't marry him. Such a thought fills me with a big black cloud, I could never make him happy, not as he should be. There. That's it.

You know what a decent fella he is, I don't need to preach to the converted do I? So please realise that if I go through with this wedding I am destroying both of our lives. It's not easy for me to not show up at my own wedding but I know that it's the best thing and, the only thing to do.

I don't have the guts to tell him myself. I know that you can do it much more decently, with words that I could never come up with, so that he understands that it's for the best.

My phone is switched off but I'll switch it back on soon so please leave me a message and I will call you.

I love you my dear friend and without you I would go through with this charade and, consequently, destroy the future of a decent human being.

I'm sorry, from the bottom of my heart, I'm sorry.

Friends always. See you soon.
Nora   xxxxx

The letter is no longer relevant and I know that Mandy won't tell anyone she's found it but she keeps reading the letter over and over again. I feel her agitation.

I can feel her soul jumping around, it's a whole mix of anger, irritation, pain and sorrow. I try to calm her, fill the room with peace. I turn to Original Sid for help, he's so cool, he gives a shrug and lets me know that we have to leave her to go through these emotions, we can't interfere in this one.

But, we'll be there to comfort her once she's processed her own despair.

Two years later

Time has no meaning to me but despite this, since my passing I have evolved. You can't hide from yourself over here, it's not even a consideration. I've seen how clumsy I lived my life and I need to make amends. I look forward to having another chance.

How easy it all should have been but I, *me*, created stumbling blocks which certainly made no sense to life. Life truly is that simple, why do we create problems when they're not necessary? It all seems so very futile now.

I've faced up to how wrong I was, you can't escape it here, that's the way it works. I've evolved a bit more towards the goodness we all need to achieve. I've scrutinised the way I treated Bigsy, a decent man, I was a coward and afraid to act out the truth. Why? Because I was weak and thought more of my own self, how I would be perceived by those around me. I can tell you, with absolute certainty, that there really is a right way and a wrong way to go about every single thing in life and in no way is it as complicated as we all think it is.

Now, I'm so eager to put things right, to live a life in a body, with more awareness of my responsibilities and to try and spread this joy and love I have inside of me, I'm nearly ready, and raring to go.

The world has so much destruction and pointless violence, such unkindness for each other, it's useless and causes misery to the soul. But, unfortunately, the world is a place where peace, in all its completeness, will never reign. Hate and prejudice have taken it too far down a road of destruction, it's now too fractured, too engrossed in self-loathing and the judging of fellow human beings to ever recover.

The world is populated by a cluster of wretched souls who blame everyone else and who never take responsibility for their own actions; it is up to each one to answer for their own wrong-doings and to face up to their own conscience, to decide what is wrong and what is right, and to live by that.

Hurting someone, emotionally, causing them to panic and rethink their life is sometimes the best favour you could do for them, if only they would realise that when that pain hits them, if they then heed their inner senses, in time, they will see the reason why it happened, and it will all make sense. A new road waits for them.

But wallow in self-pity and moan *"Why me?"* will only create more misery.

It's as simple as that.

Armed with this knowledge I'm returning. I'm very excited and the planning is precise.

But, as Original Sid tells me; I need to be really strong because once I get back into the atmosphere my soul won't be as aware as it is now, I need to work really hard to remember all I've learnt and listen to what it tells me. I have to trust my soul and the words which jump into my head, I have to follow my gut instinct with confidence. Even when, sometimes, it's easier to allow apathy to take control; I will need to take time and listen to my inner voice.

The main thing, Original Sid says, is to know the difference between right and wrong and stick to the rules of the soul which I know to be true.

I went to the wedding a while back, they were all there; my previous mum and dad, Sid and all the rest of them.

Mandy and Mark – their names were always well suited. I filled that church with all the love and energy I could muster, I heard my old mum tell Sid that she could feel me close, giving my blessing to the pair of them. How right she was.

They're going to have a really good life, I know it. I sensed from Original Sid that within a short time they'll move to Australia, they'll be living close to Sid and his new wife. I could not have given Bigsy the joy he now has in his life, I would never have loved him, properly, and allowed his soul to grow. Mandy is the perfect person for him, together, they will achieve goodness which will radiate out and touch others in a positive way.

Had I lived, and married him, he would never have known how good it feels to be loved.

Today

Original Sid is with me at the hospital. We're waiting.

I've been in and out of that womb throughout the whole pregnancy, it's amazing in there. I'm aware of my soul and at the same time I know I'm a growing baby. It's warm, it's secure, actually, it is the best of both worlds.

Early on, I tried to persuade Original Sid to join me in the womb, but he still has work to do. He wants to be there to greet my old mum when she goes over, in a few weeks' time.

I asked him to come later and be my sibling, or even cousin but he said no, he has other karma which needs to be resolved, along a different path to mine. He did say though, that we would certainly meet at some point in the new life, probably very briefly, he said.

'Such as?' I asked.

'I don't know,' he shrugged, 'when the time is right and

fitting, for the reason why it has to be. Then we will meet again.'

'Such as?' I need more from him.

'When we both need a small reassurance, to reboot our soul. I don't know … It could be that we sit next to each other on a train journey. We will recognise a familiar affinity, we will talk like old friends, then we both will go our separate ways. It will be only a fleeting moment compared to our lifetime, but it will have a lasting impact.'

'I wish I knew for sure when and where…' I need a definite assurance that he will be there. 'What if I mess it up and am nothing but a disappointment to my parents? I want to make up for all the pain I caused but how can I make sure this is the right time to return?'

'At this stage, if you decide that the moment is not right for you to return, then you should pull out. The choice is yours. But be aware of the utter pain and heartache this would cause. Are you prepared for that?'

'I decided to return so that I can help to erase the pain I have already caused, not create more. Yes, I am ready.'

Now, the moment has arrived, Original Sid tells me I need to get back in there, sharpish.

I say a strange farewell to my old uncle and go into the womb ready to be born into the world. I hear a familiar voice, my old mum is here in the hospital, she's telling Mandy not to be afraid, she's kissing her head, just like I used to do, and then Mandy screams and I do too.

I feel a pain in my back, something is thumping it with, what seems to be, a wooden mallet. I'm being pushed down a tight tunnel, the pain is excruciating, I want it to stop, it's crushing me, please make it stop but no, it gets worse the further down I go, it becomes tighter, a vice is clamping my head, the pain is unbearable, I'm not sure I can take it…

I scream. The cold air makes me yell in terror, my secure home has dissolved into a vastness where I feel a weight so heavy it pulls me down. Gravity. I had forgotten its weariness.

Strangely enough, my cries of confusion brings joy to my parents, they smile at my arrival, whilst all I feel is panic and fear.

****

'It's a girl.' The nurse holds the newborn aloft for all to see.

'A girl! We have a daughter.' Tears flow down Mandy's cheeks, she struggles to sit up, she holds out her arms, 'please let me have her, let me hold my baby.'

Her husband Mark cups his daughter's head in his hand, so tenderly he kisses the downy head, he swears to himself that nothing, ever, will harm this child. He takes her from the nurse and hands her to his wife.

Mandy holds the bundle close to her breast; she runs a finger over the warm round cheek.

'Hello Nora, I'm your mummy and this is your daddy, you are *so* loved,' Mandy bends her head to kiss her daughter for the first time.

Mark puts his arm around his wife; the beauty of life engulfs him and takes his breath away.

In all his days he has never known such joy and happiness.

2. History Of A Stick

'This is a really lovely piece. Can you tell me a bit about it?' The antique dealer looked closely at the silver mark on the collar. 'How did this wonderful walking cane come into your possession?'

'I bought it from a car boot sale, a few weeks ago.' The young man replied.

'These car boot sales...' The dealer sighed, he really should make time to get up at the crack of dawn one Sunday and go to one himself. 'Do you mind telling me what you paid for it?'

'Four pounds.' The young man ran his large calloused hand over his blond, close-shaved head. He wasn't interested in antiques but even to his basic knowledge he thought it would be worth more than what he paid for it. Whatever he could get for it would go towards the stag do. A dozen of them were going to Las Vegas in a couple of weeks.

'Well, let me tell you a bit about this cane, it's a very interesting piece...'

The young man wasn't at all interested in the story, he just wanted to know how much it was worth, and if the dealer would pay him the full rate for it.

'At first glance it seems to be a late nineteenth century walking cane. The wood is Malacca,' the dealer fondly stroked the wooden shaft of the cane.

The seller felt slightly uncomfortable.

'I'm pretty sure that, originally, this was a sword cane.' The dealer looked at the seller, 'or sword stick,' he explained further. 'This,' he ran his finger over the large round stone jutting out of the top, 'is tiger's eye and the collar is sterling silver.' He looked closely at the decorative silver clasp holding the stone in place. 'Further down the shaft you can see it has been sealed with silver wire.' The dealer pointed this out to the seller who tried to look interested. 'I believe that this has been done to encapsulate the sword inside.'

'So do you think there's a sword still inside?' The seller asked, showing a bit more animation at the thought of it being more than a boring old walking stick.

'Yes. Yes I do.'

'How much do you think it's worth?' The seller had another couple of antique dealers he would visit in the old market town - if this one didn't offer a fair sum. He'd done a bit of research on the internet and would be happy to get two hundred pounds for it.

'Five hundred fifty pounds,' the dealer replied.

'Oh…' the seller tried to act cool. 'Would you be interested in buying it then?'

'Yes. It is the sort of thing I could find a buyer for, yes.'

'You'll give me five hundred and fifty for it?' The seller could barely contain his joy.

'I could give you four hundred.' The dealer glanced at the dismay on the sellers face. 'Five hundred fifty is its worth, that's what I would sell it on for after I have cleaned it up.' The dealer already had a buyer in mind and he knew he could get at least six hundred for it, but he was waiting for the seller to start haggling the price, he was prepared to pay five hundred for it. 'I have to leave room for my expenses and a bit of profit.' He tried to goad him into hammering out a deal.

The seller had no idea he should start to haggle with the dealer and he accepted the offer of four hundred there and then.

Already on the phone as he left the antique shop, the young man laughed loudly to his mate on the other end. 'Oh yes! We

21

have another four hundred quid for the pot!' The tables in Las Vegas would benefit from his find.

<u>New Year's Day 1900</u>

If William Gardner had been a cautious man he would have taken the news that the standing stone at Stonehenge - which had fallen over the day before, the last day of the century – as a bad omen. But William Gardner was not a man to be frivolous with his emotions.

His intention, the previous day, had been to make it look like a burglary. Nothing more than that. But it had gone horribly wrong.

London was steadily becoming a safer place to live, more so than it had been earlier in the century. With growing numbers joining the Metropolitan Police the force's presence was becoming more visually obvious on the streets of the capital. Although unrest was still prevalent amongst the residents, which was probably due to the shadow of Jack the Ripper the year before, which still hung in each stench-filled dark alley of the East End.
   Still, the very presence of the police force made for a more confident feeling of safety, even though pickpocketing, housebreakers, and murder was still an everyday way of life in the capital.

Already, for months, William Gardner had lived with torment foaming like an ulcer inside him. His staid and unrepentant demeanour etched on his stony face; his refined waxed moustache matched the perfection of his hair, sleek with Rowland's Macassar oil. He dressed like the perfect Victorian gentleman that he believed he was. His façade gave nothing away of the turmoil mounting inside of him.

Today, Monday, the first day of January 1900, he felt a small sense of relief that the house in Eaton Square would not be lost after all. The upper class address - their home - which had been handed over to him by his wife's family upon his marriage to their daughter Rose, did not have the grandeur of its neighbours in Belgravia or Mayfair. He knew that his wife's family were not pleased with her choice of husband and the annual allowance they gave reflected this, it wasn't sufficient for their upkeep and it forced him to continue working in the accounting firm he owned with his business partner Edward Faulkes.

He felt their resentment wash over him every time they visited for afternoon tea. Rose had given birth to his two children and her parents doted on them, it made William feel inferior.

William was a gambler, a poker player. He couldn't pinpoint the exact moment it had all started to go downhill, the precise second when it had taken a hold eluded him. The whisky and the opiates stripped him of every common sense he had when he sat at the table. The feel of the cards fanned out in his hand made him invincible, the stirring in his loins filled him with urges which would be fulfilled by Anna-Marie later in the evening.

Since the birth of their last child, Rose had denied him of any intimacy within their marriage, she had done her duty and produced both a boy and a girl and so, as far as she was concerned, sex was no longer necessary. William had a collection of pornographic magazines which he read in the privacy of his bedroom and which he kept in a box beneath the bed. He had every copy of *The Pearl* ever published and when publication stopped, after the authorities closed it down because of its obscenity, he re-read them over and over again. Now he had moved on to Anna-Marie – a living, breathing, prostitute.

Strapped against his stomach, giving him a paunch which was hidden beneath his Melton cloth overcoat, there against his clammy flesh sat more than two thousand pounds. Enough to pay off his gambling debt and, therefore, retrieve the deeds to the house.

He walked rapidly along the street towards King's Road, his walking cane tapping the ground as he marched.

When he reached the house he furtively looked around him, if he caught the sight of someone he knew, he would have walked on. But his darting eyes saw no-one he recognised. William held onto the metal railings as he made his way down the awkward steps to the basement of the townhouse. He held the cane in his hand and tapped the tiger's eye three times against the door. The door opened almost immediately and he disappeared into the darkness.

When he came out, William's paunch had disappeared and the deeds to the house sat safely inside his coat. A smile curled one corner of his mouth as he walked back along King's Road, he wanted to laugh with the solace which now replaced the toxic scum in his innards. The house was safe, if he hadn't been able to repay the money by noon on this very first day of the century, he would have been destroyed, he would have lost everything.

Before going to the office he had two more things to do. He

checked his pocket watch, it was still only nine thirty, he would be at the office by eleven - if he walked quickly.

In the street behind Victoria station he found the small shop he was looking for. The bell above the door clanged loudly as he entered.

'Good morning sir, how may I assist you today?' The salesman asked William.

'I understand that you do repairs,' William held up his cane to show the item for repair.

'Yes, indeed we do sir. May I ask what the problem is?' William handed the cane over to the man who inspected the original steel tip on the bottom of the stick, 'the ferrule is still in good condition…' he pressed the silver button on the shaft and pulled out the sword, 'as good as new!' he smiled and slid it back in until the button clicked back into place.

'I need you to seal over the button so that it looks like a normal walking cane, so that the blade is locked inside…' William felt his neck getting red, 'this is my favourite cane but you know what it's like with small children…my wife, she is concerned, she thinks that my son may think of it as a toy and harm himself. As I do not wish to part with it I would prefer to seal it.'

The man laughed, 'Oh, I understand completely. My wife is very particular about the items I take into our home too.' The man looked closely at the cane. 'I think the best thing would be to wrap silver wire around the shaft; that will stop the child harming himself.'

'Will it still resemble a sword cane?'

'I'm afraid, to the untrained eye, it will look like an ordinary walking cane sir.' The salesman had a look of sympathy on his face.

William sighed, 'Oh never mind, I suppose that's to be expected. At least I will still have my beloved father's last gift to me,' he lied.

The salesman gave a look to say that he understood. 'Do not worry sir, I will make the cane so perfect your emotional attachment will not be disturbed in any way.'

'Thank you. I appreciate that. When will it be ready for collection?'

'One week on Wednesday, if that is agreeable?'

'Indeed it is. I will return next week.'

'You do not have to concern yourself sir, we will deliver it to your home once the work is done.'

'No. No, that is not necessary. My wife is in need of a new umbrella so I will find out her preference and purchase one of your fine examples when I return for my cane.'

'That would be a pleasure sir,' his eyes glinted, he would get his very best umbrellas ready for his return. 'Now, if I may just take your details?'

'Certainly. My name is James Stamford.'

'Thank you, sir. Please be assured that my workmanship will be perfect.'

'I have no worries. Thank you for your time and I shall see you next week, on Wednesday.'

William strode swiftly, making his way to a small street behind Covent Garden. The door into the pawnbroker's shop was at the side, down a rather dingy and noxious alleyway. If this shop did not have what he needed he would have to purchase a brand new one, he would prefer a walking cane which had had some use, he wanted no suspicion upon him.

Luck was on his side, he shook his head – where was that luck when he needed it yesterday…and at the gambling table?

The pawnbroker looked at the well-dressed customer; he'd had them all in his shop, he didn't judge, he boxed their goods and paid less than their worth. Most times, it was the posh ones who never came back for their stuff. The thick gold rings on the pawnbroker's fingers intertwined as he clasped his hands tightly.

'I've mislaid my walking cane.' William spoke abruptly, he felt naked and undressed without a cane in his hand.

'Did you retrace your steps sir?' the pawnbroker asked.

'I don't have time I have a very important meeting and I cannot walk the street without a cane. What do you have?'

'I do, as it happens, have a few which I can show you.' He turned to a cupboard behind him and reached inside for half a dozen canes.

William scanned them quickly. He smiled as he picked up an ebonised cane, the brass ferrule had some knocks and dents which was good, but it was the tiger's eye handle mounted into a clasp of silver which decided it for him. This was his style and no-one would comment on it.

'I'll take this one. Thank you.'

William checked his pocket watch, he would need to move quickly to get to the office by eleven.

****

William knocked on the door of Turnbull's the Solicitors before opening it and popping his head into the office. He was never over-friendly with them, sometimes they worked with the same clients and so it was inevitable to have contact. Today, he wanted to have witness to his arrival.

'I would like to wish you all a very good New Year, in to the new century we go!' William smiled as he spoke.

'Thank you and likewise.' Arthur Turnbull walked across the room with his hand outstretched, ready to shake. 'We shall have to catch up for a drink and toast the new century in an appropriate manner.'

'Yes, yes we must indeed.' William turned to leave, he cocked his head to one side, 'no noise from above…perhaps my partner hasn't arrived at his desk yet.'

'No, I've been here since nine and he's not arrived yet.' The young solicitor's apprentice was glad to have the chance to join in and have an opinion in the adult conversation.

'Oh well, he'll be here in his own good time. We arranged to meet at eleven…perhaps he's having a bit of a sleep after too many whiskies for the celebrations yester evening.'

'That's most likely,' the young lad laughed.

'Right, I'll be off and get started. Good New Year to you all.'

William knew that it was now crucial that his every action was perfect and believable. He walked up the flight of wooden stairs knowing that each thud of his foot on a stair would reverberate into the office below.

He reached the landing outside his office, the frosted glass in the door had been smashed, straight through the company name of *Faulkes & Gardner, Accountants*. Smashed yesterday by the tiger's eye handle on his cane, which was now in a small, unimportant backstreet shop and which couldn't be traced.

'What the…?' he called loudly, so that they could hear downstairs. He pushed open the shattered door with his foot and yelled even louder, 'Good God man, what's happened?' William stomped his way back to the top of stairs and yelled for Arthur Turnbull and his apprentice; 'Help! Go get the police!'

****

'He's not been dead long.' The police officer announced as he covered the body of Edward Faulkes with a white sheet.

'How do you know that?' William Gardner wanted to tell him he was wrong, it was nearly twenty hours ago that he thrust the blade of his sword into his heart.

'His body's not cold enough, it's still got warmth to it.'

'But it can't have…'

'Why's that then sir?'

'When I arrived – just before eleven this morning – I first paid a visit to the solicitors downstairs, I wanted to wish them a good New Year… they had been here since nine this morning and heard nothing. Surely, my partner would have alerted them had he been alive?'

'Looks like he bled to death. Slowly. He would have lost consciousness but still breathing, till the end…was he in the habit of arriving at the office early?'

'Sometimes, yes. We would both be here at whatever time necessary to make sure clients' needs were met…we arranged to meet at eleven, he didn't say that he needed to be here early.' If this was the route the police were to take it would make it much easier for William.

'He must have opened that safe for the thief, and who knows? Maybe there was a tussle and he got stabbed. It's all speculation at the moment sir, we need to get the crack team on the case and they'll have it sorted in no time. Now, if you can tell me how much money would have been in the safe?'

'I do not know the precise figure – I can let you know that

once I look through the receipt book – but I would estimate there to have been in excess of four thousand pounds.'

The police officer lowered his pencil, his jaw dropped and he gaped stupidly at William Gardner.

'That was not normal, but we were holding that amount for two separate companies who are currently in the process of selling.' William thought better of saying anything more, a large amount of the money was from one of their clients who wished to squirrel away a small fund to support his mistress.

Once he had paid off his gambling debt William still had two thousand pounds left over and which he had hidden under his bed with his magazines. It would be a buffer to get him out of ever being in the same situation again, in the future.

Killing Edward was not part of the plan but he had arrived at the office as William was taking the money from the safe.

Edward tried to take the money back, he shouldn't have done that, he really shouldn't have. He threatened to tell Rose and their clients unless William put the money back. That was the mistake Edward made. If he had turned around and walked away he would still be alive, they could have sorted this whole darn mess out, but no, the obstinate buffoon of a man had to interfere.

William looked at the small rotund man with his bald head and thick glasses, one punch and he could knock his business partner out, he was desperate, he *had* to have that money to pay his debt, he couldn't allow Edward to stop him, he would be ruined.

Edward lunged at him, trying to grab the money. They had a struggle and Edward bit William's wrist, he was like a rabid dog. William kicked and beat his head with his fist but Edward grabbed him around the waist, he tried to grapple him to the floor. William reached for his cane resting against the desk, he pressed the silver button and the blade shot free of the casing, he was panicking, he just lashed out and the blade slid through Edward's clothes and flesh like a knife into warm butter.

Edward staggered backwards before he crumpled to the floor in slow motion. William stood watching him, a dying man gasping for his breath, he bent down and wiped the blood clean from his sword on Edward's trousers before slipping it back inside the cane.

He closed the office door behind him and locked it, he then ran at the door and rammed his shoulder against the frame, but it didn't budge. He wanted to make it look like a break-in so he tried again and this time the door splintered and flew open, William staggered through the doorway, his arms flew out to stop himself falling and his cane smashed the glass.

With one last look at his partner on the floor, not moving, blood trickling over the rug, he turned and went down the stairs. By the time he reached the front door he was calm. A strange reaction for a man who had just committed murder.

It was only now, as he stood in the middle of the carnage with the policeman chattering ten to the dozen that he realised he hadn't locked the front door when he left, or kicked it in as he had planned. It was a minor detail and they probably wouldn't even pick up on it. He wouldn't worry about insignificant details, they didn't have enough brains between them to figure it out.

****

Tuesday, the following morning, and William hadn't been back to the office, the police said he wasn't allowed until they had done everything they needed to.

He was in the drawing room reading the newspaper when the maid came in to say the police were in the hall and would like a word with him.

'Show them in Hilary and bring us some tea will you.' He told the maid.

'Yes sir.'

'Good morning sir, I apologise for dropping in unannounced but we'd like to go over a couple of things with you if we may?'

'Most certainly, whatever I can do to help catch this man…' he allowed his voice to trail away.

The two policemen sat down opposite William. 'When was the last time you saw Mr Faulkes?'

William sighed, 'it was on Friday. Normally we would be in the office on Saturday of course, but what with all the end of century celebrations we decided to close for the weekend, we arranged a meeting for eleven o'clock on Monday morning. Edward had no immediate family so he planned to take a day trip to Southend on Saturday and on Sunday he would spend the day with his landlady and her family.'

'Yes, his landlady confirmed that.'

'Did she say what time he went to the office?'

'He went on Sunday and didn't return home.' The officer told him as he stared without blinking at him.

'Did she say what he was doing going to the office on Sunday?'

'He went for a pack of playing cards.'

William looked at the policeman. 'Playing cards?'

'Yes, apparently they were playing parlour games and the dog, somehow, got hold of the cards they planned to play with and chewed the ruddy things to bits. They all found this hilariously funny, they were all in high spirits and Mr Faulkes announced that he would go and get some more cards as you, sir, had a couple of packs in your desk. Is that correct?' The police knew it was correct as they had since found them in his desk drawer.

'Yes, that's correct. I like to play *patience*, it relieves stress.'

'We believe that the burglar arrived before his victim and that the front door was not locked, in fact we *know* it wasn't locked because when the solicitor's young apprentice arrived on Monday morning it was already unlocked with no sign of forced entry. The apprentice had been the last one in the building on Saturday, and he can't have locked up behind him. He got a right clip round the ear from Mr Turnbull for it, I saw him do it myself...which means, the burglar had a clean entry.'

William felt he wanted to keep quiet, so easily he could say something out of turn.

'We've spoken to your clients,' the other policeman spoke for the first time. 'We can be one hundred percent certain that they are not involved in the robbery as they were both out of the area at the time.'

'Whoever killed Mr Faulkes, they left him for dead but it took several hours for him to die. Poor beggar...'

William felt exceedingly uncomfortable. 'Can I get you a brandy?' He went across the room and poured himself a drink.

'Not for us thank you sir.'

William gulped his drink and poured another.

'We are still looking for the murder weapon which, we believe, to be a sword of some sort, with a blade of about 25 inches.'

'Well that won't be easy to hide, will it?' William got up and poured another brandy.

'I think that's all for now sir, but we would like to have a word with your wife if she is available.'

'My wife? What can she tell you? Nothing! Why do you need to speak to her?'

'Sometimes we get a different viewpoint on things. It's nothing important but we need to keep our records straight.'

'Well, if you must…I will see if she is available. One moment gentlemen, please.'

****

'We won't keep you long Mrs Gardner, we just have a few questions for you.'

'Not a problem officer, the sooner you find the person responsible for this horrendous incident the better.'

'Mrs Gardner, can you tell us what you bought your husband for his Christmas gift.'

'Of course, I bought him a portable silver moustache protector which I had engraved with his name, and the date.'

'Do you know where it is, presently?'

'I think it may be in his overcoat pocket, in its own little case. On Sunday morning the children were playing with it, I scolded them and told them that their father would be angry if he found them playing with it. I bought it for him to carry round with him – the wax in his moustache melts with the steam and heat of the tea, this little gadget sits on any cup, a marvellous thing – my eldest child returned it to the case and put it in his father's overcoat pocket.'

'Did your husband leave the house on Sunday?'

'Yes, he leaves the house every day at some point. I'm not sure what time he left but he was home at nine o'clock because we had supper together before retiring for the night.'

'Does your husband own a sword Mrs Gardner?'

'Not as far as I know, he does have a collection of walking

canes and some of them have inside compartments to hold a drinking flask and I think perhaps one may have a sword, but that's not a *real* sword, is it? Would you like to see for yourself?'

'Yes, if we may.'

Rose Gardner led the policemen into the large hallway and guided them to the stand with a cluster of walking canes.

'I think it may be this one.' She pointed to the Tiger's eye.

The policeman took it out of the stand and inspected it carefully. 'No, this is a normal walking stick.' He took another and another before finding one with an ivory top which released a blade. 'Hey presto,' he winked to his colleague.

'Would you mind checking your husband's overcoat for the portable moustache protector?'

'Of course.' Rose went to the coat stand and searched every pocket of every coat on the stand. She shrugged as she looked at the policemen, 'it's not there…'

'Don't worry, it was a longshot. We will take this cane and return it as soon as we can.'

****

Wednesday 3rd January 1900. The police returned to the house and arrested William Gardner for the murder of his business partner Edward Faulkes.

When they moved Edward's body, they found, clutched in his hand, a small case containing a sterling silver moustache protector, engraved with: *William Gardner, Christmas 1899 from Rose with affection.*

Inside the lid of the case, before his slow death, Edward Faulkes had managed to use the edge of the trinket to scroll, in blood, *Wm.Gardner killed me.*

During the hearing, the defence pointed out that the murderer must have smashed the office door *after* fatally wounding Edward Faulkes as glass and splinters of wood covered the body yet none were found on the floor beneath him.

A large sum of money was found in the bedroom of Mr Gardner but neither the murder weapon nor the remaining money was ever recovered.

Thursday 10th May 1900, William Gardner was hanged for the murder of Edward Faulkes.

****

1902 – The shopkeeper in Victoria tried to trace James Stamford, the owner of the cane with the tiger's eye and sealed over button, but the man had disappeared from the face of the earth. He waited nearly two years before he sold the item to recover his cost of the silver. And there, its journey began.

****

One hundred and ten years later, as a stag party of twelve young men boarded their plane to Las Vegas the antique dealer found a buyer for the cane he had bought for four hundred pounds, he sold it on, making himself a profit of £350. It's true provenance never revealed itself.

The gambling tables in Vegas took back the £400, along with every other penny the young men had between them.

It is almost certain that, if the current owner of the cane happens to be a gambling man, then his fortune is in danger of being forever lost.

3. Dawn French Bought My Lava Lamp

Philip frowned with discomfort as he walked over to his wife. Margo was leaning forward in her seat, her back straight and angled toward the computer screen, her head moved slightly as her eyes darted back and forth over the icons on eBay. Philip felt the familiar burning at the side of his knee as he moved towards her. Sometimes, without notice, the pain of a thousand bee stings would shoot through his leg, the pain would be so bad it would make his eyes water and his breath rattle in his throat.

'Any more takers?' he asked his wife.

'Well, we're getting there. Not as much as we would have liked but, it's all better than nothing.' Margo said the words with a hint of false elation. She continued to stare at the monitor, 'at least everything has a bid on it.' She turned to her husband with a big smile which didn't hide the forced joyfulness of her voice.

Philip peered over her shoulder to see for himself. 'I'd have thought that that Swan Carlton Teapot set would have more than nine quid on it by now!' he tutted in dismay.

'It's difficult, that dent on the side of the teapot takes away its value a bit. Anyway,' Margo gave a reassuring pat to his hand resting on her shoulder, 'don't get despondent, there's still another half hour to go, there could be a mass bidding war in the last few seconds, a dozen snipers waiting in the background, ready to throw their bid in the pot!'

'That's my childhood, that is, that teapot.' He said the words softly, to himself.

'We had one too. I think it was *the* teapot to have in the Fifties.'

Margo moved the cursor down the page to see each of their

items for sale on the auction site, the dented teapot set was the item with the highest bid.

'What about the Lava Lamp? Surely that should be into double figures?'

'Nope, six quid.'

'Six flaming quid? For an original Mathmos? It's scandalous!'

Margo remained silent. It pained her to sell the lamp. Silly as it seemed, it was a memory as clear as a picture in one of the photo albums in the dresser, a representation of the day when she egressed into adulthood. The lamp was a treasure she had loved every day for the last forty-odd years; but how could she whinge and cling on to it when Philip had already allowed his own treasured bits 'n' bobs to be sold?

Over the last few months all cupboards, closets, boxes in the attic and crates in the shed had been ransacked to help pay their bills, fill the car with petrol and buy groceries.

****

It was the summer of 1968 and with the money she had been given for her twenty-first birthday, Margo took the train to London. With her handbag swinging in her hand and a smile on her lovely young face, she made her way to King's Road. This was the place she had read about, she had seen pictures of it in magazines and on TV, it was the *only* place in London she wanted to be, *the* place to buy her new, grown up, persona. She may even stop off at the Kenco coffee house and read a fashion magazine as she sipped an Italian frothy coffee, she may even see some famous people…what if one of the Beatles or Rolling Stones were window shopping and saw her, even smiled at her? Her excitement felt like an electric current running up and down her arms and surging through her stomach.

Her mind raced with pictures of the things she would buy, the famous singers and models she may see, the smile never left her face as she stood on the platform waiting for the train to London. She fancied herself in skin tight, knee-high boots, like those she'd seen Twiggy wearing in *Jackie*, she wanted the purple Biba dress with a flutter of feathers on the shoulders to go with them, she had cut the picture of Twiggy in the whole ensemble from the magazine, it was folded neatly inside her handbag.

She wanted to show just what a trendy dresser she was. Nearly every Saturday night Margo and her best friend would go to The Bop, it cost a shilling to get in and everyone knew it as *Bop for a Bob!* There, they would dance to the latest hits played through two huge speakers on the stage. In a couple of weeks though, Procol Harum were booked to play. The girls already had their tickets and played *A Whiter Shade Of Pale* over and over again on the record player, it would be a night for dressing up in much finer clothes. Normally, Margo would have chosen something already in her wardrobe to wear but, there was someone she wanted to impress. A handsome lad, who, someone had told her, was called Philip. She often caught him looking at her from across the room or as she walked by on her way to the ladies, and when they had eye contact he would smile at her.

That was the worst thing he could have done; the fact that he even acknowledged her created the blood to erupt, heat to explode in her face, she blushed and her face burned, she knew her cheeks were bright red and she was mortified. Margo would lower her head to allow her long hair to fall and hide her pretty face, so that he wouldn't see her blushing. On the dancefloor she would keep her back towards him.

Twiggy-boots and a feathery purple Biba dress would give her the confidence to walk with her head high, without blushing. Dressed like that, dressed in her clothes from the swinging King's Road at the Procol Harum gig, she would smile back at him.

Margo tried to hide her naïve stares as she watched in awe at the wonderful creatures walking up and down the Chelsea street, they would disappear inside darkened doorways where music blared with the latest hits. If she heard the Monkees or a bit of Tamla Motown coming out onto the street from one of the doorways, she promised herself, then, she would go inside. Margo had only ever shopped in department stores; *Boutiques* were alien to her, they were a darkened world were only the confident and famous people shopped for their clothes.

And so she walked, up and down, listening for *The Happening* or something just as familiar, to filter through the door which would allow her the confidence to enter. Walking back down the other side of the road she thought that, perhaps, she should go to Carnaby Street instead.

Margo stopped at a window where the display wasn't as chic as the others.

It had an array of floppy hats, beads and embroidered Afghan coats set against a background of metallic spirals twirling down from the ceiling. It wasn't the merchandise which interested her, it was the mesmerising display of lamps on the floor. Each lamp was shaped like a spaceship with globs of colour floating slowly, up and down, hypnotically they flowed, the balls of colour joined together then separated to become a regenerated shape.

Margo had never seen anything so beautiful, so serene, in her life.

Some of the lamps had a translucent background liquid with purple or green globs floating around, the one she stood gazing at - a magnet to her eyes - had yellow liquid with bright orange spheres slowly sailing up and down; entrancing her.

Without hesitation she walked up the two steps to the doorway and through the beaded curtain into the shop. The smell was strange; a mix of joss sticks, strong tobacco and raw Afghan coats.

'Hello,' Margo's lack of confidence had disappeared as she approached a young man with hair down to his elbows, he was sat with his legs crossed, swinging in a pod chair suspended from the ceiling.

'Hi,' he replied before taking a puff on his fat roll-up.

Her eyes darted around the shop looking for the display of lamps so that she could choose the one she wanted.

She knew, without a doubt, that she could not go home without one.

'What you looking for?' the man asked in a slow voice.

'Those lamps, in the window…' Margo walked over to a table painted with bright sunflowers, daisies and psychedelic swirls, a display of colourful beads and headbands encircled the lamp, glowing and flowing in the middle of the table. She knew that if she could have such a lamp she would never ask for anything again.

'Lava lamps? They're cool man.'

'They're beautiful.' she whispered as she watched its slow, sensual dance on the table.

'We don't sell 'em though.' He held his breath as he spoke, before slowly allowing smoke to exhale through his pursed lips.

'Oh!' her head snapped up in disappointment. 'Do you know where I can buy one?'

'Go back, up towards Sloane Square, and there, on the other side of the road; Their window display's full of 'em, you can't miss it.'

Margo thanked him and turned to go.

'Tell 'em *CandyMan* sent ye,' the hippy called after her, 'I'll get my commission then!'

She caught the train home to Hertford, carefully carrying her lamp and swinging her handbag which held her purchases from Biba; some blue eye shadow and a small bottle of perfume – it was all she could afford after buying the lamp, she would have to make do with the clothes in her wardrobe.

*****

'Oh, here we go! Here we go!' Margo sang excitedly, 'twenty minutes to go and we have a bidding war on the lamp.' She had become drawn into the excitement of the bids but her heart still wept at parting with it. She had checked out the price for a new one which would set someone back to the tune of nearly £70, she knew that hers wouldn't bring that, the liquid had lost its vibrant yellow hue, it was now a bit murky, the orange wax had faded but still, it was a magical thing and the warm glow it beamed was soft and comforting – she had put all these details into the description.

An original Mathmos Astro Lava Lamp from the swinging sixties – bought on the King's Road. She didn't add; *this simple lamp means more to me than you can ever imagine.*

''How much is it now?' Philip called from the other room, it took a couple of seconds before his joints, which were riddled with arthritis, allowed his legs to move. He'd been made redundant from his job in the distribution warehouse at the large packaging firm, three years ago.

He knew his job wasn't redundant; they'd renamed his role and taken someone else on, a young lad who could jump in and out of the forklift truck with the back legs of a young kitten. Philip had worked there for twenty-five years and they gave him a full year's salary, tax free, to go.

'Twenty quid.' Margo called back in a distracted voice, she was checking out the profile of the bidder which interested her more.

Time and time again she had asked herself the same question; how on earth had they got themselves into this situation?

They'd never been rich, they always took their summer holidays along the coast, in Cornwall. They saved what bit they could and they had managed to buy their council house. At this time in their life, what with Philip's redundancy money and the bit of money which she earned from cleaning at the local school, it would have been more than sufficient to see them through until they could take their pension.

But they had got above their station hadn't they?

Margo chided herself; it was she who had egged him into it, it was her fault, all of this. They thought that they were business folk and could make it work, when all it had done was dissolve their money, like acid, and left them with virtually nothing.

Margo had always made chocolate, she was the original pioneer of blending it with strange ingredients, this was long before those chocolate connoisseurs came jumping onto the TV screen, filling up the supermarket shelves with their specialist treats.

Everyone had told her that she should make it professionally and sell it. Margo poo-pooed their suggestions; who would want to buy her chocolate?

So, through the years she continued to make her slabs of white chocolate with swirls of beetroot juice running through it like veins, milk chocolate with crunchy peppercorns, dark chocolate with shredded carrot and ginger and the most wonderful of all; pureed avocado, olive oil, crunchy sea salt and a dusting of cayenne, all enfolded by dark, best quality 70% from Ecuador.

Back then, when she first started making the chocolate, these were just too weird for anyone to consider buying. And then the fashionistas arrived on the scene demanding chilli chocolate, sea salt and all the other strange combinations which, Margo had already been making for years.

With Philip's redundancy pay plus the bit they had saved, and a few thousand from remortgaging their house, they built an L-shaped annexe at the end of their long garden which doubled up as a workshop. They had it fitted out with a stainless steel kitchen and work benches, heated and air conditioned, living room, bathroom, bedroom and an office. They bought everything they needed to get the business up and running and stocked it with the very best chocolate Belgium had to offer.

They had a website built - professionally done mindst you - and they paid a handsome fee to a marketing company to promote *Cocoa-Choco-lot*. It was an exciting time; that thrill of having a business, doing something that you love filled Margo with a new wave of life.

The orders came in, not large orders, just small ones which didn't even allow them to break-even. Friends and family bought the chocolate but Margo felt bad about taking their money, she had always given it to them as gifts or treats, how could she now start to charge them?

'*Are you sure?*' they would ask when she refused their money, '*tsk, yes of course, put your money away...*'

When their money pot began to show a significant hole and the marketing company turned out to be less than useless, Margo decided to start selling her chocolate at craft fairs, she kept the price low and affordable, but more often than not, it didn't even allow her to recuperate the cost of the stand.

She wandered round the town square in Hertford, handing out leaflets advertising their website and giving out free samples. She took to Facebook and flashed up special offers for first time buyers. But no-one came. Traffic to their website was no more than five visits a week.

No matter how much she Tweeted and recited the quotes of family and friends; it was as though *Cocoa-Choco-lot* was invisible to the outside world. Margo sat for hours searching the web for help and advice, for that magic link which would allow their website to be seen. It felt as though she was struggling through a wall of treacle.

People were more than happy to take the free samples she offered and they all told her that they loved the chocolate she made, no-one ever turned their nose up at yet another piece of her edible delights. Margo felt that whichever way she turned, whatever way she tried, there was some secret code evading her, a magical switch which, if only she could find it, would open the floodgates and bring people to their site.

And still she continued to walk around the town square each Saturday, handing out leaflets and free samples of chocolate which people took, ate and asked for more, the same faces would search her out each week for their free sample. And still, each day she prayed that she would find that elusive code which would turn their lives back onto the road; the one of security which they once knew.

****

'Dawn French bought my Lava lamp.' Margo stood in front of Philip and said the words quietly, in a controlled voice which masked the joy and exuberance detonating inside her heart.

'Dawn French? Are you sure?' Philip pressed the button on the side of his chair - he called it his Bond ejector seat - the chair tilted sufficiently for him to stand up, still with difficulty but, it was better with the tilt, than without. He followed his wife back to the computer. 'These internet people take-on all kinds of personalities when they're hiding behind the veil of the internet, maybe it's a Dawn French fan, or wannabe…?' he continued as he followed her.

'No, it's not. I've been looking through her feedback from other sellers. Listen to this, right?' Margo clenched her fists and gave a squeal as she scrolled through the feedback, it was worth losing her beloved lamp for it to be bought by *Miss.French* which was the name the buyer called herself. 'Here we are…*Thanks Dawn! & a pleasure to deal with you*…so we know she's called Dawn, then we have; *I totally admire your work & thrilled to deal with you,* another one says: *Hope to deal again with Miss French, now fllwing U on Twitter*…what do you notice about these comments Philip?'

'Well, yes, I have to say it seems indeed, to be *the* Dawn French.'

'That's not normal feedback, is it? That's more like people fawning over a famous person.' Margo jumped up and hugged her husband.

'Can you see what she's actually bought from these people?'

he asked, thinking it may give away more clues and confirm her identity.

'Unfortunately, no. All her buys are marked as *private*. But you know what this means don't you?'

Philip looked at her quizzically.

'This is that link we need, the code I've been looking for to send *Cocoa-Choco-lot* ballistic!'

'Aha, I'm getting your drift,' he said, even though he hadn't a clue where it was leading.

'Everyone knows that Dawn loves chocolate. So, all we have to do is fill-up all the spare space in the box with chocolate, and a few choice leaflets, I'll pop a note in there asking that if she likes my chocolate –'

'Which I'm sure she will,' Philip interjected.

'Then would she be so kind as to Tweet about it and mention it on her Facebook page.'

'As we could do with any help she can give!' Philip laughed.

Margo and Philip stood in the middle of the room clenching each other's hands; Philip reached out to his lovely wife, he pulled her close to his body, he inhaled deeply and sighed.

'A Tweet from Dawn French will solve all our problems, just one Tweet – that's all we ask of her.' Philip whispered into his wife's soft hair.

'As soon as she pays it'll bring up her details, but in the meantime, we can start getting it packed up and making it all nice for her.'

The pain of losing her lamp had been eradicated; Margo remembered that day in the King's Road, London in 1968; whoever would have thought what it would lead to?

Each ping on their smartphone, telling them a payment had been made into their PayPal account, had them laughing and squealing to see if it was from Miss.French.

'Don't worry, it'll come.' Philip told his wife.

'I'm not worried my love, she's got 100% positive feedback, it's Saturday, she's probably out shopping.'

'Or maybe doing a matinée in the West End?'

'How very exciting,' Margo gathered all the items, everything had sold, she put them in order to match them up with the payments made, so that she could prepare to post them. 'Do you know what I think?' she asked her husband.

'What do you think, you wonderful woman you?'

'I think we should splash out a bit, why don't we pop to the supermarket for one of those meal deals they have on, you get a starter, main, pudding and a bottle of wine for a tenner, what do you think?'

'Come on, let's go and treat ourselves, and maybe a cake or something to celebrate?'

'I think we can choose a cake of some sort in the meal deal. Let's see what we get to choose from first.'

'I've seen those on offer but never taken much notice before.' Philip pushed his feet into his wide slip-ons.

Margo bent down to pull the Velcro over the top of his shoes; she patted his feet and stood up, 'there you go my handsome lover.' She checked to make sure her purse was in her handbag, 'Righty-oh, are you ready?'

****

'Let's not get ahead of ourselves!' Philip laughed as they walked through the car park back to their car, holding hands as always.

''I can't help it!' Margo gave a little skip, 'I'm worried that it'll become too big for me to handle, we might have to sell, maybe some *chocolatiefied* Gordon Ramsey will come along in a few months and offer us a small fortune to take it over.'

'If it pays the debts and gives us enough to get by on, then that would be a dream come true.'

'I've been looking for that vital key for so, so, long and, all the time it was there – in my Lava lamp.'

'We can buy you a dozen Lava lamps in all different colours!' Philip moved to kiss his wife's cheek as she opened the boot where he carefully placed the carrier bag. He fleetingly wondered why Dawn French didn't just buy a new Lava lamp, 'I'm looking forward to that wine,' he said as he closed the boot and dismissed the thought; she probably had the need for an authentic prop in one of her sketches, he told himself.

'The whole meal is a veritable feast, we can pretend we're out on a date,' she chuckled cheekily which made Philip laugh out loud.

'We've got some candles, haven't we?'

'Yes we do have some candles, Mr Romantic.' Margo tapped his bottom lightly.

****

Philip poured the chilled white wine and invited his wife to sit down, he held the chair for her and rubbed her shoulders as she settled herself in.

The beep of a PayPal payment pinged on the phone, 'Oh quick, quick!' Margo looked around wondering where they'd left the phone, they only had one mobile between them; they had no need for two.

Philip handed her the phone, 'I can't see a darned thing, where are my glasses?' he patted his pockets and looked around the room before shrugging and taking the seat opposite his wife.

'No, it's not Dawn.' Margo sighed as she checked the phone, 'that's the last of the other payments though, so the next ping we get we will know, it's definitely Dawn!'

'She's probably gone out for drinks with the cast, or dinner after her matinée.' Philip told her knowingly.

'How exciting it all is.' She raised her glass and blew a kiss across the table.

****

They were both just about to climb into bed when the phone pinged, heralding the payment from Miss.French.

'I dare not look.'

Philip put on his glasses to read the screen, *you have received a payment from Miss.French,* Philip reached out to his wife and pulled her close, 'come on, come on,' he rubbed her back to soothe the breath heaving through her body, relief of the last couple of years released itself, their worries were surely over.

'We only want her to like the chocolate and send one single solitary Tweet, to all her fans…I'd even *give* her the lamp as a gift…'

'Let's get back down those stairs and fire up the computer again, otherwise you'll never get to sleep tonight!' Philip took charge of the situation.

They knew the computer would take a good few minutes to start up so, in the meantime, they made themselves a mug of hot chocolate, complete with a sprinkle of white chocolate and cranberry shavings.

Patiently they waited. The smile on Margo's face eradicated

all the angst she'd been through; that look of worry which had recently extinguished the sparkle in her eyes, had now gone.

Margo landed on the *Order Details* page; her eyes went straight left, to the delivery address column.

'Damn it, I've left my glasses upstairs, where does she live Margo?'

'Hull.'

'Hull?'

'In a convent.'

A laugh blurted out from Philip's lips, 'what?'

Margo tuned to face him, 'Dawn French - is Sister Monica.'

Notification of an email from Miss.French popped up. She left the page and went to log on to her emails.

'Well I never!' Philip shook his head, 'that's not very Christian-like is it? A nun impersonating a well-known figure, pretending to be a comedienne, deceiving folk. You don't think she's a stalker do you? Are you sure it's not her?' He asked, confused by it all, 'I mean she *was* in that vicar of Dibley. I think she did a nun sketch as well…I seem to recall.'

Margo ignored him and read through the email:

Dear PhilArgo
I am absolutely thrilled to have won this lava lamp. Every Tuesday I go along to a local school and read stories to children with learning difficulties. I have wanted a lava lamp for ages as I think the children will benefit from the calmness it evokes, they'll love watching it gently bubbling away as I read to them. I think they will focus on it and feel calm, these children are very special, they exist in a different world to you and I and, I believe this lamp will help and thrill them enormously.
Please may I ask that when leaving feedback you do not refer

51

to my religious name or my vocation, as this, strangely enough, seems to cause a problem with some people. My baptismal name is Dawn French (yes, yes I know!) I would appreciate your understanding in this matter.
Thank you again and please know that the children will benefit more than you can ever imagine from this lamp.

Kind regards

Dawn French
(Sister Monica)

Margo read the email out to her husband, her voice was flat and empty; her world had been pricked by a missile and deflated before her eyes.

'Do you want me to re-pack the box?' Philip asked her softly.

'No. No, leave the chocolate in there for the children.' Margo squeezed his hand and smiled, her throat was tight and her chest ached.

Philip stood up and went to get the box anyway, he would take out the flyers and the note she had written asking Dawn to Tweet.

For a few hours he had seen his beloved wife come alive again, and now, in an instant it had gone.

'You know what? I've been thinking, for a while now…' Philip sat on the arm of the chair and picked up her hand, he kissed it before cupping it tightly in both of his.

'What have you been thinking, my love?' She rested her head against him, despite his aging years she could still feel the strength and firmness of his body.

'It's not all doom and gloom, all is not lost, we've still got a bit of equity left in this house, and this place is getting too much for us anyway, what with that big garden…why don't we sell up? We'd get a decent price, especially as it comes with a granny cottage at the bottom of the garden. We'd have enough to buy a small place, or even one of those mobile park homes. We would have enough to live a decent life; we could even go to Cornwall or, somewhere?'

'Cut our losses and start again?'

'Yes, exactly! We've still got a lot more than a lot of folk out there.' Philip looked at his wife closely, 'We'd be close to the sea, or not even Cornwall, we could look around, maybe the Lakes?'

'Yes. Let's look into it. Tomorrow, we can look at the options tomorrow.' Margo had no heart to be enthusiastic about his suggestion, not yet, but for once she would listen to her husband and follow his lead, instead of running off with flouncy ideas of her own.

'Come, let's get to bed and tomorrow we'll start again.' Philip stood up and reached out his hand for her. 'We could look at Devon as well.'

Margo smiled at her husband, she knew that he was right, and in her heart of hearts she knew that she would get excited about it, eventually, but first, she had to get over the disappointment of her failure.

'Just one Tweet from Dawn French, that's all it would have taken.' Margo bit her lip and took her husband's outstretched hand. He smiled at her and she knew that their new start would work out just fine. And, more importantly, the love of this man was all she needed in her life.

4. Peculiar Ways

I spent most of my school life stood in the corridor.

They were dull and lacking imagination, were my teachers. My school report never changed, year upon year it always repeated itself with the same old words; *Trevor disrupts the class…he'll never amount to anything…he needs to curb his peculiar ways.*

Luckily, my mam couldn't read and so, until the day she died, she was proud of the glowing reports which I read out to her. I sang my praises, but I didn't go over the top, no, I knew my limits. Mam would sign it to say she'd read it, her own name was the only thing she could write; *Edna Wright*. It confused her when I told her that "Wright" was different to "write" she couldn't quite get the gist of it, so we gave up and carried on as we always had done.

She loved me did my mam, a lot.

And I loved her, just as much.

It was just the two of us at home, I once asked her about me dad - she told me I didn't have one and that it was good enough for Jesus, so it was good enough for me too. I never asked about him again.

I was different when I was at home, I was myself. School was the disruption, not me.

My mam left our two-up two-down house at ten past six every morning; she biked to the big house where she cleaned the stairs and the bathrooms until three o'clock in the afternoon, six days a week. She had Sunday off and then we'd go to mass together.

I loved Sunday, it was the best day of the week for me, I wasn't keen on the going to mass bit though, I fidgeted too much, mam said .

No, I loved Sunday because it was bath day.

****

'Did you get any perks today ma?' I would ask her each evening when I got home from school.

'Aye, I've got a bit of bread 'n' butter pudding for ye tea.' She would say, or some other such delicacy she'd brought home with her.

I would rub my hands in glee at the thought of the lovely grub, before going to the sink to wash my hands and face.

'What's this?' I remember once asking in disgust, when she put a bowl of pale liquid stuff in front of me. The smell was bland and unenticing; like a cold, damp warehouse.

'Parsnip soup. I forgot to mention they had a load of parsnips spare today…' Mam would give me that look which I knew well, the one that said *don't you dare turn your nose up young man, otherwise tha'll be no pudding…*

Still, to this day, I don't like parsnip soup, not even the gastronomique version which the Michelin star restaurant, in the hills near Valbonne, serves.

Anyway, as I was saying…Friday was the best day for the perk and if it came with a bit of fish for our tea or a slice of sponge cake bulging with strawberry jam, which the housekeeper sent (specially for me), she had a soft spot for me, me mam said, then I called it a *Sperks* day; "S" for *special*. I'd have given them all up, them other perks, if I had to, except the one on Friday.

Because this was the day my mam brought home the bits of soap. Them who lived in the house were fussy blighters, once the bar of soap lost its original shape and was smaller than the length of the piece of string, it had to be replaced with a new bar. She was supposed to measure it with a tape measure, me mam was, but she couldn't figure it out so I cut a piece of string with a knot on each end which was the right size, so that when she put the string around the middle of the bar; if both knots could touch each other, then she knew she had to replace the soap. String was right handy in our house; I blackened a couple of lengths of it with coal dust and used it for our shoe laces, that, and a bit of newspaper stuffed inside the toe, stopped them shoes from flopping off my feet.

After our tea, at about six o'clock, me mam would hand me the thing I'd been waiting for. She would wrap it in a clean hanky. To this day, I can still feel the cotton weave of those handkerchiefs against my fingertips, the soap would have dried by the time she got home and it would be clinging tight to the material.

I had a routine, I like routine - always have. First off, for a minute or so I'd feel the shape of the soap resting in the palm of my hand, then I'd raise my cupped hand, cradling the perk, to my nose; the scent came slowly, like a breeze, like a gentle cloud floating over me, filling my head with pictures of their scent. Scents are pictures and emotions, not words. I had two which I loved the best.

The first one, I called *Field Marshall*. A handsome man with a black moustache, who sat upon a leather saddle, which creaked as he moved. His horse was dark brown and shone with the sun, together they would walk through a lemon grove. The Field Marshall was strong willed and had no fear in him, he loved to sit back each evening, on the terrace, with a glass of gin and tonic, he would watch as the sun went down over the hills of far-away India.

I didn't know if they even had lemon groves in India, but that didn't matter.

My most favourite I called *Buttoned-up;* because when it was winter and I wanted to go outside and play mam would say "c*ome on, let's get you buttoned up...*" It was like being snuggled in a warm cocoon when my mam held me close; I felt safe and loved, that soap had a softness which filled my nostrils and comforted me.

I was secure and no matter what them teachers said, I knew, they were wrong – I *would* become someone, I had no idea how it would work out, but *something* would happen to lead me to that elusive bit of me which, at that time, I couldn't quite understand. *Buttoned-up* was a blanket of love and the knowing, that it would one day happen. It was my faith in the future.

I had bits of soap all over t'place; inside my pillow case, in the pockets of my trousers and I'd even put them inside the newspaper in my shoes. I'd have the hanky which mam had carried home with last week's perk, in my pocket, I'd take it out when the teacher was rabbiting on about something which held no interest to me whatsoever, I'd hold it to my nose and I'd *know*, that one day I'd be in that place where I belonged.

The kids in my class had strange smells; I would get up close to sniff them. They'd look at me angrily and shout to Miss that I was licking them, which, of course, was totally untrue; I was inhaling their scent. One day Miss said that I was acting like a dog and I should stop. Since that day, they all started calling me *the dog*, it didn't bother me, I was the cleanest kid in class, I never had that musty smell of dirty hair and stale bed linen which clung to them and gagged at the back of my throat when they came too close.

I realise now, that I should have done science and art at school, I would have discovered my compartment. Art and science are bed-mates in the world of perfume. I don't think they did science at my school though, if they did, they kept it a secret from me.

That's why I loved Sunday, bath day. I would take the newest bar of soap and climb into the tub of hot water. I would rub it between my hands and cover my face with the lather, I would even clasp the bar of soap tightly inside my flannel and suck on it; my taste buds catapulted a storm of pictures which moved like a film all around me.

One day I went to the chemist with my mam; she wanted a bottle of calamine lotion for the gnat bites which covered my legs one summer. I thought I'd landed in the hereafter…as soon as I walked through the door, a trillion isms attacked me, lifting me up and flying me around on wings of iridescent, soft citrus gossamer and this time I heard music, I really did: a chorus which made the hairs on my body stand on end. I had found nirvana.

When we came out and entered the world of warm tarmac, I told my mam that I would like to own a chemist shop when I grew up. She was really pleased with that.

****

I never got many birthday cards or presents, but on my fifteenth birthday I got the best present I could ever want. Mam was at work when the morning post came. The letter from school made me laugh out loud and dance a jig around our small parlour; they didn't want me to go back after the summer holidays, they felt that I was beyond help, I was ignorant and it was best I try my hand at finding work as a manual labourer instead of wasting their time returning to school.

When she came home, I told my mam that I'd decided not to stay on at school for my O-levels; I was going to find myself a job. I could see that she wasn't thrilled by my announcement, she asked me three times if I was sure about my decision and three times I told her yes, I was absolutely sure. 'Alright,' she said as she walked to the sink to swill the teapot out, 'but the school's going to be mighty disappointed.'

A couple of days later my mam came home and I asked if she had any perks.

'No, there's none today son. The house is full of relatives from all over t'place. Like gannets they are, they eat everything in sight. Wasteful 'n' all…they take a bite of t'apple and then chuck it away. Why they want to come up north for their summer holidays when they've got that big place in France? It beats me…'

This was the same every year, sometimes my mam would have easy days, that's when the owners went abroad for a few weeks, but when all the family congregated on the edge of the Yorkshire Dales - cause that's where we lived then –well, it were mayhem, not only for us but for the whole town.

Anyway, she said she had no perks but, she did, she had the next best thing to the Friday perk.

'But there's one thing…' she said as she poured hot water into the teapot and I could feel the scented steam from the leaves filling my head with the picture of an old steam train straining to get itself up a steep mountain.

'Oh aye?' I said.

'They be looking for a young un to work, for t'next few

weeks, cleaning all them cars that are filling up the front of t'house. Seymour's got his work cut out for him, ferrying 'em a-hither-and-a-tither.'

My mam turned to look at me, 'I thought it might be summat for you?'

I remember my heart thumped hard – would I be able to go inside that house? Discover the source of *Field Marshall* and *Buttoned-up*?

'I know it ain't suited to your skills, you don't need all your learning for it but…well, just something to tide you over the summer?'

'Tell 'em yes mam! Tomorrow, I'll come with ye!'

'Well, I said I'd ask…he's a bit of a hard task master though, is Seymour.'

'What way?' I was willing to put up with anything to get in that house.

'He's a right stickler for speaking proper, he's always correcting me, I *do* try…'

'I know you do ma.' I didn't like it when anyone picked on her because she couldn't read or write, or because of the way she spoke. Sometimes we'd sit on a night trying to talk all posh and try to speak without chopping our words up, it ended up the pair of us blabbering on in a right strange way. Even now, people will comment on my accent, they say I speak with a nice accent with intermittent lapses.

Funny that, 'cos I speak French like a proper aristocrat.

Right, where was I? Oh aye…I got this job cleaning cars up at the big house, I even got to drive them, from the front of the house to the back. I didn't dare tell Seymour
I'd never even been in a car before, never mind driven one. Luckily there was a young lad who worked in the stables, and

he showed me how they worked.

When I was old enough I took my test and passed first time – that were without a single lesson in me life! That meant I could be a bit of a chauffeur when Seymour was too busy. I didn't get to go inside that house for three years, it cut me in two, so it did. But when I did finally get to go inside, it tore me to pieces.

'Trevor!' Elaine, the old housekeeper came running out of the house shouting for me, 'Trevor, come quick – it's your mum.' She was posher than us, was Elaine.

I dropped everything and without a second thought I ran inside the house.

'Here!' Elaine led the way, 'we've called for an ambulance, it should be here soon.'

'Has she fallen down the stairs?' I asked, not sure why I thought that but it was probably due to the fact that I had just glanced the biggest staircase I had ever seen in my life, it looked terrifying.

'I don't know…she just fell in a heap, on the floor.'

A young lass – I knew she was one of the daughters - was knelt on the floor with me mam's head in her lap, my mam looked pale and frail, I knelt down by her side and took hold of her hand – it was small and bony, I rubbed her knuckles. Where had all that plumpness gone? Why had her body become so skinny without me noticing?

'What is it ma? Eh?' I stroked her face, she gave a little smile and said, 'I'm so proud of you Trevor, you're the best son a mother could have. I love you son. If I had a dozen hearts, I couldn't love you more.'

I could feel a tight lump gripping the back of me throat. 'I love you too mam…come on, pull yourself together lass…' I wanted to yell at her not to leave me, 'I know it's mid-week but I'll pick us up a fish supper for our tea tonight, eh shall I?' My mam smiled and pressed my hand against her lips.

She'd already gone by the time the ambulance arrived. I didn't know what to do with myself. I was in bits, I really was. Eighteen year old I were, my heart shattered with physical pain, I was alone without my beloved mother. I thought I would never laugh again, in my life.

Crikey, even now it still gets to me… pfst, never mind, let's move on…

They were decent people, them who owned the house. They paid for my mam's funeral and made a right good day of it for her. Elaine made her favourite cakes and we even sat in one of the big rooms playing the piano and singing. It were a lovely day, for a lovely lady – my mam.

Like I said, they were decent folk and I reckon they wanted to do right by my mam and look after me. I hadn't long passed my driving test when they asked me to drive one of the cars down to their house in France, I'd be full up of luggage, it'd take me near on four days to make the journey, catching the boat from Dover, stopping overnight at different places. I have to admit I was a bit scared at the thought of it all and didn't know how I'd manage it.

They gave me a map of France and together, me and Seymour, planned the route. I asked Elaine to save me some soap to take with me. One inhale of *Buttoned-up* and my mam would be with me, right beside me in that car, all the way.

****

As you've probably guessed, I'd never been to France. In fact, I'd never been further south than Skipton. I had to laugh, as I drove through our small market town, on my way to Dover, I stopped at a zebra crossing to let Miss Turner, my old headmistress, cross the road. I papped the horn as she started to cross, I smiled and waved at her; her face was a picture, seeing me behind the wheel of a Bentley ... I laughed my head off. Miss Turner never had a particularly pleasant scent to her either.

France, oh France! What an explosion of head pictures it was for me. As I got nearer to my destination in Mougins, I knew I was home. I belonged.

****

That was near on sixty years ago, and I've never been back home to Yorkshire since.

A lot has happened in them years. It's all down to fate isn't it? It has to be that, there's no other explanation as to how I got to where I *had* to be, where my strange and *peculiar* ways were greeted with adulation.

I get a bit cross really, when I think of them teachers and what they told me; that I would never make anything of myself. They were short sighted and judgmental, if they'd have taken the time to mentor me a bit, they would have noticed that I had something to offer, but I suppose it was beyond their scope. I guess they did me a favour, kicking me out on my fifteenth birthday.

I stayed on in Mougins once the family all left to traipse back to England. They had a couple who lived in the house and looked after it all year round, an English couple but we had a bit of a to-do with them.

He was knocking-off the young cleaner who came in twice a

week; his wife found them at it in the laundry room and threatened to shoot them both. All hell broke loose and we tried to keep it quiet, but the wronged wife was having none of it. Out into the garden she went, yelling and shouting. Off she went like a washer-woman possessed, storming over to the pool; where the family were sat having a quiet chat over breakfast. She was waving his underpants like a flag of war as she ran across that garden.

The owners were not impressed and they let it be known in no uncertain terms. It seemed they'd had a bit of trouble with them before, they'd somehow managed to break some handles on a bureau which, reportedly, had once belonged to Napoleon Bonaparte (I've since learned that almost every antique in France likes to link its provenance to: "once belonging to NB"). Anyway, that's not the point, the point is, they replaced the handles with cheap wooden ones from a DIY store and didn't tell the owners. It was noticed though, and then they had to own up.

So, what with that in mind, you can imagine that this little episode of a dalliance was the last straw and the pair of them were sent packing.

That's how come I stayed on to look after the place. You can't leave a house like that empty and unattended.

We took on a young woman from Libya who had a small child, they lived close by, she came in to clean and do bits around the house and brought her baby with her and I did all the other stuff to keep that house in good shape.

I was in my element there; the scent on a morning, depending on the season, started my day off like fuel in a car. I went on mini tours around the Perfumeries in Grasse, I bought books and sat for ten hours without moving, engrossed in the pages of the history of perfume making. I had a lot of freedom - which was one of the perks of my job - I must stress though and let you know, that I always took my position seriously, and when the family came over I worked every day, solidly from dawn till bedtime, non-stop. But once they left, well, I took care of the house rightly and proper then I was free to do that which ruled my heart and soul.

It was on one of my trips to the oldest perfumery in Grasse, I'd been living in France for nearly five years, when the door I had been searching for opened. I came across a small tour of English ladies, from Thirsk would you believe, we got chatting and then discussing the perfumes.

'This one smells the same as this one.' One of the ladies held two bottles aloft. I, naturally, butted in when I heard her words.

'I think you will find that this one,' I pointed to one of the bottles, 'has a strong scent of tree bark and moss, whereas this one,' I pointed to the other bottle, 'has an overall scent of freshly sawed wood.'

The woman shrugged, 'they smell the same to me.'

How could I argue? You either *get* subtleness or, if not, then it's a useless argument. I smiled at her instead; perhaps a bit patronising of me but, well, take art for example…I was once in Antibes at the Musee Picasso when I overheard a couple discussing his work... Ah, but before I go on, I have to say that I may be a perfume snob but art is something else, I would never get involved in those conversations which you hear when walking slowly round a gallery, you've probably heard them yourself, where they discuss in hushed tones how the artist felt whilst painting a eucalyptus tree or what the woman he drew sat at the table with a glass of absinthe was thinking –

I would not dare pertain to know what went on in his head whilst he painted something, unless of course he documented it. In fact, I find it embarrassing when I hear such conversations going on, rather pretentious.

Getting back on track…Not sure what I was about to say…

****

The comment I made to the women, about the tree bark and wood, was overheard. As I was leaving the perfumery a gentle, a polite man, approached me and asked if he could have a word with me, I thought I must be in trouble, had I said something out of turn? I hoped that they weren't about to ban me, that's the trouble when those who were meant to teach you as a kid, only inflicted an inferiority complex into your psyche, making you think that you have nothing worthwhile to give society, my mam knew different of course, but that's a mother's love and duty isn't it?

Thinking that I'd overstepped the mark and was about to get a bit of a pasting for it, I followed this chap to his office where another two people sat behind a big shiny desk, they sat me down in a squashy leather chair, the sort directors in big offices have.

'Trevor,' Jean-Yves said my name in a very elegant way, I liked it. 'Would you mind helping us in a bit of research we are doing?'

'With perfumes?'

'Ah yes, of course with perfumes.'

'What would you like me to do?' I was mightily relieved that I wasn't in trouble after all.

They wheeled a trolley over to me and gave me a phial of liquid and asked me to tell them what I thought of it.

'This is sadness, this is what tears of grief would smell like if they had a scent but then…there comes a hint of sunrise. This is rather flowery, this is not my most favourite of scents…it's a Citroen Deux Chevaux without the wheels.'

The group said nothing, nor did they react. They handed me a tray with boxes of wool and cotton for me to clear my nose of the scent but I shook my head, I can automatically change my senses. I took the next phial.

'To the regular customer this could be mistaken for a well-known perfume, but this one has a slight overdose of lily of the valley, only a fraction, but still, a fraction too much which spoils it.' I told them.

Even though I say it myself, the team were speechless, and actually, so was I. I hadn't a clue where all this knowledge came from – I just *knew* it.

'Trevor,' he said again, 'how would you like to come and join us, work at our perfumery, here in Grasse?'

Well, I didn't need to be asked twice, I can tell you.

****

I felt bad when I phoned the big house in Yorkshire to tell them I was moving on, I promised them that I would stay on until they found the perfect guardians for the house in Mougins, no matter how long it took.

I did the preliminary meet-ups with various couples, I was getting a bit despondent to tell you the truth, after six weeks of seeing people-upon-people who gave false smiles and said just the right thing at the right time, I'd nearly given up hope of finding the right pair. Then in came a middle-aged couple and I knew the search was over. The owners came over from England and confirmed that yes, these two were perfect.

I packed the few bits I had and moved to an apartment in Grasse.

****

I've always loved life but, early on, when I was a kid, I wasn't sure how it would pan out. Now that I've spent most of my life in the perfume trade, here in Grasse, I wish I'd known then that I had nowt to fear for the future.

I don't see it as a gift, it's my joy in life. When I was working my apprenticeship with Jean-Yves, he would show me off to the others in our trade, *I have the best nose in the business working for me*, he would tell them. I would turn away, all that talk was nonsense and I didn't like it, but still he would brag and flaunt my skills. I just wanted to keep in the background and get on with it.

I got offers from other houses which I didn't even consider, at the time. But once I'd found my feet, it took near-on ten years mindst you, I decided to go out on my own. I'm still friendly with Jean-Yves and all them over there, where I started, there were no hard feelings when I left.

I started small, then it went mad. I bought this lovely big house right on top of the hill overlooking Provence; *Le Beau Champ*.

You need to come here, you really do – we do tours you know – and the views, the perfume…I live on the top floor and everything goes on in the rest of the house.

I don't do much work nowadays. Now and then I'll have moments of lucidness when I'm young and *know my stuff,* as they say, but I forget that I'm an old man now, and some days I can't seem to remember yesterday very well.

One thing I do know is that my time, since the day I left

school, has been everything a man with peculiar ways could want. I dread to think how my life would have been if I hadn't been brought, by fate, to France, I shudder to think of how imprisoned in my own essence I would have been, with no escape. Can you imagine? It makes me shudder just to think of it.

Le Beau Champ signature perfume is the best-selling of them all, it took me a couple of trials but I got it…I darn well got it, spot on.

We couldn't really call it *Buttoned-Up*. Not quite chic enough is it? So we just translated it into French and voila! Boutonné was born.

I got the company lawyer to draw up a contract with the precise ingredients, you may not know this, but many perfume houses change the ingredients of your favourite scent, have you ever thought "blimey this doesn't smell like I remember it"? That's because they reformulate it, and it's never the same, it annoys me, really it does…My memory isn't up to scratch but my smell is as vivid as ever. I can take in a scent which I haven't smelt for years, yet it takes me back there, in an instant.

At least the formula for Boutonné will never ever change, not even after I'm dead.

I'm going out for dinner this evening, I'm looking forward to it, we're going - when I say *we* I'm talking about my team from downstairs - we're going to a lovely restaurant in the hills, we go there every few weeks. We say it's a work do but it's not really, we have good food and laugh a lot. The restaurant have the most incredible olive oils, some are like a spitfire accelerating through the senses.

I have a lovely housekeeper called Ifrah, she's a wonder, she really is. Ifrah does a bit downstairs as well, with the tours, she knows the ins and outs of the perfume world and I reckon, like me, she was born with the gift of it all. She is able to answer the most obscure questions from the visitors, I don't know where she gets her mastery of our world from but she is amazing and I'd be lost without her.

****

'Ah, Ifrah, there you are. Have you put my clothes out for dinner?'

'You're eating at home this evening Trevor.'

'It's our dinner in the hills tonight…'

'No, that was *last* Thursday, we all went there last week.'

'Oh, really? How disappointing…'

Time is such a strange thing, isn't it? Sometimes, quite often in fact, I try to figure out if something I thought had happened, or was said to me, was something I dreamt or thought about or whether it did actually happen. I have no idea. It's as though I have a mist in my head and I can't see through it.

Last week I met a visitor and got chatting to them, an American lady whose mother had once worked for Elvis Presley. I was thrilled to hear her tales and couldn't wait to tell my mam. For a few seconds I really thought she was still alive. It took a while for me to fathom out where we all were.

I put the milk in the cupboard and a bowl of cornflakes in the fridge and then firmly believed, because I couldn't see the bowl of cereal that I had eaten my breakfast. What a silly old fool I have become.

****

'Ifrah! Do you happen to know where my notebook is? I can't seem to find it and I want to write some thoughts down, before I forget them.'

'As it happens, I remember you having it when you sat out on the terrace this morning, having your coffee. I'll go and look for it.'

'Thank you my dear. What would I do without you Ifrah?'

'What would *I* do without *you* Trevor?'

'We are both children of fortunate circumstances, in an unfortunate world.'

Ifrah smiled at the old man and knew just what he meant.

5. The Whistleblower

Whistleblowing policy:
The purpose of such a policy is to encourage employees to raise their concerns with regard malpractice or misconduct of which they become aware in the company. The employee's (whistleblower) identity will be safeguarded by the company and every effort will be made to protect the employee from any reprisals.

Should the allegation of malpractice or misconduct be substantiated, appropriate disciplinary action will be taken against the employee(s) which may result in dismissal and termination of contract.

The whistleblower must not use this policy as a cover to act maliciously or make false allegations. The concern raised must be in good faith and not for any personal gain or malignant purpose.

Should the allegation prove to be a malicious use of the whistleblowing policy, appropriate disciplinary action will be taken against the whistleblower(s) which may result in dismissal and termination of contract.

~~~~

'Jake? Please call me as soon as you get this message.' Tanya exhaled loudly before ending the call. She looked around the office at her colleagues, which one had it been? Who had sent the photos to her manager? Everyone looked normal, no-one seemed, in any way, guilty of pulling off such a stunt.

That's all it was, a stunt. Whoever took those photos had no idea of the situation which they thought they had seen, they made a dangerous assumption which could end up destroying her.

The past couple of weeks hadn't been the best in her life, whether the Gods were looking in another direction or the moon in her stars was passing through a phase of destruction, she had no idea, but no matter what she tried to do it all seemed to be backfiring into a cloud of black dust.

If she could pinpoint the moment of descent it would be the day her best friend, Marion Walker left *Vivid Creative Designs & Construction*.

Tanya was a Tender & Proposal Executive – a job she loved, whilst Marion had worked in Customer Services - which she hated. Who would enjoy being on the phone the whole day having to be nice to people who moaned because their neighbour had just been quoted a few hundred pounds less for the same attic conversion that they had done two years ago? Not many that's for sure and which was evident from the high turnover of staff in the department. Marion had stuck it for longer than most people but now she had the chance to move on. She had found herself a job as a PA for the director of a small company on the other side of town.

'I'm going to miss you so much!' Tanya hugged her friend tightly.

'Oh, I'll miss you too,' Marion hugged her, just as tightly, back. 'But, it's not going to be the end of our friendship, is it?'

'No, I know, but I can't just walk over to the other building and have a quick chat with you, who will I have lunch with?'

'We're just shifting gear on our friendship, that's all.'

Six foot tall Jake Harris, Creative Director in the same company, with abs and pecs as solid as laminate flooring, he carried the looks of a moody male model and a smile that enticed the most hardened heart to melt. A walking, living dreamboat, who was out of bounds to them all. He was taken.

Jake and Tanya had been together eighteen months, they moved in together ten months before and Tanya loved him more with every day that passed. They decided, in the beginning, that their relationship should be personal and not impact their work in any way. They hardly ever had any dealings with each other in the office anyway, they were even in different buildings, so it was easy to keep the two separate, but today, she had to talk to him.

She left the message on his phone, she knew that he had meetings most of the morning so the next person to call was Marion.

'Can you talk?' Tanya asked her friend.

'For now, the boss is on a conference call. What's up? You sound upset.'

'You won't believe it. I got called in to HR, my manager was there and they told me that they've received some disturbing information which they have to follow up.' Tanya felt her voice breaking.

'What sort of *disturbing information*?' Marion sounded slightly irritated.

'Photos of me sat in a bar with one of our clients – the *client* who is the *contact* at the *company* I happen to be working on right now with a tender for a contract – you know the strict rules we have for compliance?'

'A photo of you in a bar with this bloke can't add up to much, surely?'

'One of the photos shows him handing me a piece of paper.'

'I still don't see how this can prove anything untoward is

going on.' Marion lowered her voice.

'We're not to have any social contact with our clients. *You* know that, as well as I do. We *all* know the rules.'

'I'm confused…start the story from the beginning.'

****

Two weeks previously:

'I'll be late home tonight, hun.' Tanya took a piece of toast from the plate on the kitchen table, she tucked her blouse inside her skirt and went to the fridge to take out a yogurt for later.

'Where you off to?' Jake moved his plate so that she couldn't take the last piece of his toast.

'I'm meeting Marion in town, we're off to a bar down by the river, Marion say's it's really nice…'

'Then you must go, if Marion says so…' Jake mocked. He winked and smiled at Tanya to show he was only kidding. He got up from the table and went to kiss her cheek, 'you'd better dry your hair before you leave the house.'

'No, it's alright, it'll dry in the wind.' Tanya pulled on her jacket, picked up her bag, stroked the cat and went out the back door. 'I won't be late, I'll see you when I get home.'

'If I don't see you at work!' Jake called after her, something they said to each other whenever they left the house separately.

Tanya arrived at the bar just after five-thirty. Already it was busy, she looked for a table but the only one available was in the corner next to the door into the kitchen. She had half an hour to kill before Marion arrived so she ordered a glass of wine and hurried to get the table, she would keep her eye out for something more decently-placed.

75

For twenty minutes Tanya sat, watching without really seeing the crowd around her, her mind was filled with her future; her future with Jake.

Next year was leap year and she planned to ask him to marry her. This man was her life and her future.

Sometimes though, she worried, he seemed to be distant and cut-off from her. Of course she understood his work and the commitment he had to give his job which could be stressful but, recently, she would catch him with a far-away look on his face, she would try to pull him back to her but he would smile and get up, move away from her, with an excuse that the cat wanted to come in, or go out. The next day he would be his normal, loving, funny self, chasing her round the house and making her laugh when he smothered her body in kisses and little bites.

Tanya loved him so much. She remembered the day they went to the animal shelter and came home with Nigel the dotty cat. Tanya would have come home with a dog too; a little fella with no pedigree whatsoever, who was blind in one eye and walked like an old man on bow legs. She pleaded with Jake but, as he reasoned with her, a dog needs to have walks and exercise several times a day and they were out more often than they were home, it wouldn't be fair on the animal. Tanya thought of that little dog every day, she could only hope that he had found a loving family to care for him. When they were married, she told herself, when the children came along, then they would have dogs, cats, guinea pigs, goats in the garden and a pony in the field. That was the future she longed for, with Jake.

Those who knew her, who cared and loved her, they wished nothing less than that her dreams would come true.

Ten to six, Tanya checked her phone then placed it on the table and picked up her book, she opened it without looking and kept her eyes on the door.

The man bent down at her table and with one swift movement of his body he slipped into the chair opposite her.

'I couldn't help noticing you've been sat here for the last quarter of an hour, looking at that door…'

Tanya laughed, she guessed that this man thought that she'd been stood up. 'I'm meeting a friend, she's not due to be here until six. Do I have that aura kind of look which says I'm waiting for a man, who never arrives?'

'Well, yes,' he stretched the two words and moved his head to one side, 'something along those lines…'

'Just shows how wrong you can be.' Tanya smiled as she raised her glass and finished her wine.

'Ten minutes you say? Well, as this is the only vacant chair in the place and I've been on my feet all day, may I buy you another drink and sit here until your friend arrives?'

'Mmm,' Tanya handed him her empty glass, 'as you are so weary from your hard day's graft, I can't refuse can I?' Innocent banter was a natural part of her character.

He returned a few minutes later and placed their drinks on the table and sat down again.

'You dropped this, earlier.' He handed her a folded piece of paper which had fallen out of her book when she opened it.

'Ah, thank you – my bookmark!' Tanya went to take it from his hand which he pulled away before she had a chance to take it from him.

He picked up his glass, 'cheers!'

Tanya raised hers and they clinked glasses, as they did so he handed her the makeshift bookmark.

'I'm David, who are you?'

'Tanya.'

'So, tell me Tanya, do you come here often?' They both laughed and groaned at his crass question.

'First time for me, how about you?'

'A regular.' David clenched his lips and narrowed his eyes. 'I recognise you.'

'Do you? I don't think so…' Tanya was sure she had never seen him before.

'You drive a red Mini don't you.'

'Yes, I do…'

'The reason why I remember you is because you gave me the V sign!'

'Did I? Which way were my palms facing?'

'I pulled over to let you pass, we were both on a road with cars parked either side. Most folk put up their hand to say thank you, you gave me the peace sign.'

'I can't say I remember you, but yes, I don't do that old hand-up kind of thing, I prefer *peace-man*,' Tanya raised both hands in the V-sign. 'Palm facing outwards, unless it's some prat nearly taking off my bumper.'

'Then it's palm inward?' They both laughed. 'No, this was definitely peace. I loved it, since then I've been doing it myself.'

'Good! The more peace and goodwill we can spread dude, the better.' Tanya smiled warmly.

'Yeah, man…' David drawled in an exaggerated American accent.

Tanya's phone double-beeped, she picked it up and apologised to her drinking companion before reading the text from Marion: *SO sorry, am stuck in the office have to wait for fax from the US…could be here till midnight, pls forgive me. Can we catch up tomorrow?*

Tanya sighed.

'Bad news?' David asked.

Tanya turned her phone to show him the screen, wanting to prove that, indeed, she hadn't been stood up by some man but a girlfriend – just as she had said.

'So, does that mean you're free for the rest of the evening?' David's voice held a note of hope.

Tanya laughed, 'No, it means I can get home to my boyfriend, earlier than planned.'

****

She finally caught up with Marion the following week. Marion had found yet another bar which, she said, was not as crowded as the one by the river, and they would meet there.

It was good to be with her friend again, Tanya missed her every single day in the office and no-one, she told her, could take her place.

The last couple of days Jake had been even more remote, Tanya was getting seriously concerned, or was she being paranoid?

'I love him so much Marion, maybe he just needs to have some space? Before we moved in together he'd been living on his own, the bachelor lifestyle, for nearly two years, do you think I should give him some space?'

'Maybe you should spice things up a bit.' Marion suggested.

'Our love life is good…at least, when we *do* do it.'

'Maybe a bit of play, fun…?'

'Like what?' Tanya had some outfits she would dress up in, they had a toy box, they weren't afraid to role play and mess around, but the lid hadn't come of the boxes in quite a while now.

'I read in a magazine, about this couple, what they would do…'

'Hmm?' Tanya was all ears.

'She would change the settings on her phone so that her number didn't show up, then she sent him text messages, she would start off with something like *Hey sexy, do you wanna play?*'

'He's not going to know it's from me, is he?' Tanya couldn't see much sense in it.

'Oh of course he'll know it's from you. If you send the text whilst he's next to you on the sofa, then when he reads it he'll look at you and you can give him the come on so he knows, and then, hey yea! The fun begins.'

Tanya pulled a face, 'I'm not sure about that one.'

'What harm can it do? The magazine said that it would create supersonic passion.'

'Super*sonic* passion?' Tanya looked at her friend for clarification.

'Well, it sounds like it'd be a blast.'

'Hmm, I'll see.'

'Don't forget to change your settings first though.'

'Oh, I'm not sure Marion, it seems a bit tawdry.'

'Tsk, for goodness sake woman, tawdry, bawdry, what does it matter? Don't be such a prude!'

****

Sunday evening

The film they'd chosen from Netflix wasn't holding his attention. Tanya sat at the other end of the sofa with her legs curled underneath her body. She picked up her phone and changed the settings before sending Jake the text: *You are SO hot, wanna come and play with me?* Her phone was on silent so the whoosh of it leaving her device couldn't be heard, she continued to look through her phone, adding more pretence that it hadn't been her.

Jake's phone pinged with the incoming message, he picked it up from the arm of the sofa and read it. His face didn't change, he placed his phone face-down back on the arm.

'Who's that?' Tanya asked as he didn't react to her message.

'Just one of those service messages, wanting me to up my data and double my monthly charge.' He turned his head to smile at her, a strange smile, an ironic smile.

Tanya felt her heart thudding in her chest, maybe it hadn't gone through, so she sent another: *come on big boy I'm waiting...do you wanna know what I'm going to do to you?*

Again she sent it and continued to swipe through her phone.

Again his phone pinged and he turned it over, this time he switched it off. He tutted.

'They're persistent, aren't they, these phone companies...' she said as she watched his face as she spoke, wanting him to look at her and give her that smile which told her that he too, was playing the game and all would be well.

'Hmm.' He sighed. 'I'm going to make a coffee, do you want something?'

'Shall I put the film on pause?'

'No, you watch it.' Jake stood up, and went to the kitchen. His phone no longer sat on the arm of the chair.

Tanya stared blankly at her phone. She jumped as a reply flashed up onto the screen, she smiled, he was playing along...

I can't play now sweet pea, T is in room, will call you later, soon. Go put on that scarlet basque I bought you

She stared and she stared at the screen, devoid of all emotion, it didn't make sense. Tanya knew that she wasn't included in this game but she wasn't sure who was or what was happening.

Send T to bed. I want you for myself and I can't wait much longer she replied.

Then she sent another straight after: *red basque bit tight on heaving breast, silk stockings waiting…*
His reply shot back: *give me a couple of mins, I'll go to bathroom, God you turn me on*

Tanya waited for him to come back into the room, the thudding in her chest had turned her body into a quivering jelly, her knees were shaking.

'I'm going to skip the coffee, I'm going to go and take a shower.' He told her when he returned to the room.

'Do you want me to come up with you? I can lather you up?' Tanya felt disgusted with herself, she felt like a prostitute. How could the man she loved make her feel so dirty and degraded?

'No, you watch the film.'

After ten minutes, with her knees still shaking and her hands barely able to hold on to her phone she went upstairs. The bathroom door was closed, she could hear the cascading water of the shower, she pressed her ear against the door, his voice speaking, deep and husky, words undecipherable. Slowly and carefully Tanya turned the handle to open the door. He had locked it.

He was so engrossed in his conversation that he didn't even know she was a few feet away on the other side of the door, trying to get in.

****

Monday morning Tanya wanted to curl in a ball. She wanted to cry and turn back time, just a few hours, a couple of days...

She went to work with no idea as to what she should do. The confusion raced in her head, it was impossible, she couldn't believe that Jake was cheating on her.

When she had gone to bed last night he had been asleep already, or at least, pretending to be – she just didn't know anymore. This morning he had been his normal self, she caught him talking to the cat when she went into the kitchen. A slight upturn of relief swam through her, maybe the cat had been in the bathroom last night, he had been talking to the cat! And those text messages were all part of their game and he had been waiting for her in bed but fallen asleep because she had taken too long. The idea didn't seem ridiculous to her in the slightest.

At nine-thirty she was beginning to feel that it was all a silly mistake and that she had no reason whatsoever to worry. She would wait until they got home and she would come clean and tell him about her silly attempt to seduce him. They would laugh and all would be well.

Five minutes later, her manager came to her desk.

'Do you have a couple of minutes?' he leaned in close so as not to bring attention to either of them.

'Yes, now?'

'If you don't mind. Can you make your way over to HR, we just need a word.'

'Yes, sure.' Tanya had no idea what it was about and, at that moment she didn't particularly care.

Her manager spoke first, he thanked her for coming and told her that they had concerns about possible misconduct, and then they hit her with the allegations. They had received a confidential report that indicated malpractice involving a client she was liaising with on a tender for a massive contract. They had photographs of her meeting with the client, David White, in a bar.

They placed the photos on the table and asked her to confirm that she had met him.

Tanya confirmed that yes, she had shared a drink with the man.

The photos showed them both smiling as they clinked their glasses and, at the same time David handing her a folded piece of paper. Several more photos showed them deep in conversation, smiling, laughing, making v signs…

She was warned that the allegations were serious and breached company policy and, therefore, disciplinary procedure would now be instigated, she would receive a letter detailing the issues of the allegation and inviting her to a meeting which would be held within the next seven days.

****

Marion couldn't believe how easy it had been, she laughed incredulously at how it all fitted into place.

She'd met David White a couple of months before, when they'd got chatting in the bar, he was a natural born flirt and he enjoyed talking to women, he was handsome and cheeky with a glint and twinkle in his eye, a winning combination for any man to possess and, loaded with money from the businesses he ran – which he didn't make a big deal out of or brag about. When she first discovered who he was, the opportunity didn't realise itself until several weeks later.

Tanya first got the job of Tender and Proposal Executive, a few months before, Marion was furious, she had put her CV forward for it but she hadn't got any further than the first interview. She knew she could do that job and it was her ticket out of the awful Customer Service post which she hated, she was irked and annoyed that Tanya got it. She could have applied for Tanya's old job, they told her, but that would have been like accepting crusts off the bread.

No, she would wait and bide her time. Getting the PA job worked well and when she met David White all her eggs had fallen into the basket.

She groomed David and got to know when he would go to the bar, she could mix with him without any come back – she had no professional connection to his company. It was easy setting Tanya up, Marion knew that David would be in the bar that night, she knew that he would approach an attractive girl sat on her own and the best she could expect, as she stood at the far end, unseen through the thick crowd, would be to get a couple of photos of the two of them talking. What she didn't expect was such fantastic photos showing something which, in reality was completely different.

Whoever said *a picture tells a thousand words* had given her a ticket to her future.

And then there was Jake. Her desire for him was genuine. She had loved him for much longer than Tanya and now he was hers.

Despite how it would seem to the outside world she really didn't want to hurt Tanya, she liked her, she even cared for her.

But she cared for Jake more and she knew that he was weak for her.

****

A settlement was made and Tanya was put on garden leave for three months, after which, an amount, equivalent to ten months' salary, would be paid to her, tax free.

The allegations from the anonymous whistleblower couldn't be verified or confirmed but it held enough "evidence" which contributed to the fact that Tanya was in breach of company compliance policy. Tanya couldn't understand why they didn't contact the client who would have confirmed her side of the story.

The company felt that by removing Tanya from the company they could justify continued relations with their client and the tender could still go ahead. Therefore, a decent compromise was made to Tanya, they wanted no comeback or fuss made.

By the end of the whole charade, Tanya was happy to take the money and leave, she couldn't have continued to work for such a company, she felt that they had let her down.

****

Jake went to pieces when Tanya began to talk about the text messages, the conversation became confused and through his grovelling apologies Tanya realised that she had been set up by her best friend, Marion. She had started by apologising to him but it soon became clear that Jake was having an affair. He begged her to forgive him, he didn't love Marion, he said.

He had been weak, she had turned his head with her sexual advances.

Tanya looked at him as he tried to blame everyone but himself. At that moment it was difficult to imagine just how much she had loved him. The man she had been in love with was not the same person who now stood, snivelling, in front of her. She felt repulsed by him, the thought of him being with another woman, being with Marion, made her stomach turn.

Who had got it wrong? Had she worn those rosy glasses people often talk of, where the truth is blurred or, had Jake been a manipulator of the highest calibre? Either way and despite the pain and hurt she still felt, she was pleased that it had happened now and not at a time when the house and garden was full of children and a menagerie of animals.

She never spoke to Marion again but she answered a text which pinged on Jake's phone, she grabbed it out of his hand and read her words *I'm here for you, I always will be.* Tanya replied *Go to Hell, Bitch.* She threw the phone back to Jake and went to pack her bags.

Marion applied for, and got, the Job of Tender & Proposal Executive. It would make a full house for her if, from all her hard work she could get the David White contract, it would mean fat coffers for the company and a good bonus for her.

Jake was a broken man but she would stick around and make him whole again.

****

Two weeks later

Tanya moved back in with her parents, she could find a new place for herself or even move on to a new town. She didn't take much when she left Jake; only her clothes and bits she had taken with her in the first place and, of course, Nigel the dotty cat. The three months' garden leave would give her a chance to get herself together.

'I'm still spreading the peace.' A voice whispered in her ear.

Tanya turned in her chair to see David White standing with two glasses of wine in his hands, he placed the glasses on the table before moving into the chair opposite, he made the V sign.

'I'm glad to hear it, it's an element sadly lacking in the world today.'

'Do I detect a note of defeat?' David pursed his lips to make her laugh.

'No, not really.'

'Good, and it's good to see you again. I know you have a boyfriend,' he held his hands up in surrender, 'but I enjoyed your company…talking to you, the other week.'

'Thank you.' Tanya smiled. She should be wary of people, the two closest to her had betrayed and hurt her beyond her dreams, why should she believe this stranger? Yet his words felt sincere. 'A lot has happened these last couple of weeks. We are more connected than either of us realised – you and me.'

'Well.' David gave a little cough, 'has this got anything to do with the effects of the old hippy wacky-baccy? 'Cos you're not making much sense.'

Tanya laughed out loud, 'No!' she waited for her laughter to trickle off. 'You're David White.'

'Indeed I am, as I told you when I introduced myself.'

'No, you just said David, just as I said my name was Tanya, I didn't tell you that I am Tanya White and no, we're not related.'

'Thank goodness for that…' David shrugged his shoulders, 'I mean it would be good if we were…but my thoughts would be deemed as being indecently incorrect…'

Tanya smiled at him.

'Whoa, now hang on a minute, *the* Tanya White, who works for Vivid?'

'*Did* work for Vivid Creative…'

And so she told him the whole story.

'That is the most despicable thing I have ever heard!' David's face showed the seriousness in his voice. 'Why didn't they come to me to verify your story?'

'I asked them to but they didn't want to involve you, the client. Anyway, it's all worked out for the best because I've learned that my boyfriend and my best friend are liars and cheats.'

'I'm so sorry, I don't know how you must be feeling, I'm sorry…'

'Hey, it's not your fault!' Tanya laughed and rubbed his arm across the table, 'like I said; I really am pleased. And look,' she spread her arms wide, 'I have money in my pocket, twelve weeks' holiday and a new adventure of life to look forward to. What more could I want?'

'World peace?'

****

David White decided not to cancel the meeting he had with Vivid Creative Designs & Construction. They were certain that they would come out of the meeting with the contract all signed and sealed, he would enjoy watching them disintegrate in front of him.

The complex David was building consisted of a horseshoe-design construction with penthouse suites and high market apartments on the top three floors, the ground and first floor would be offices, a café and small exclusive boutiques. This complex, and internal design, would now be given to their competitor. Vivid were out of the picture.

'Gentlemen.' David smiled as he greeted the two partners, 'I'm sure you know why I've asked you to come over today…'

'Yes, we can guess…' they both smiled, they had a party planned for their management team, later in the afternoon – the champagne would flow – Marion had assured them that their bid couldn't be bettered in any way and she was sure the job was theirs.

'I know we could have had this conversation over the phone but I do prefer business to be done straight and face to face, don't you?'

'Oh yes, absolutely!'

'My decision, gentleman, was an easy one.' All thee smiled, two of them, somewhat conceitedly. 'And so, to put you out of your misery I am pleased to say that you have lost out to a better company.'

The smiles faded and quivered, unsure if they had heard it right or if this was a joke.

'I'm afraid gentlemen, that I couldn't possibly work with a company whose loyalty to its employees is, basically, abhorrent. Whose morals are worthless and who cannot see anything further than their bank balance. So, to play on the words of a certain group of business entrepreneurs: *you are out.*'

David White stood up and opened his office door to let the two men out.

'Thank you for coming by today. Goodbye.'

****

'Tanya? Hi, it's me, David.'

'I know who it is tootles, you're name flashed up on my

phone!'

'Well, a man's got to be sure...what are you up to this evening?'

'I thought I'd made plans to have dinner with a friend?' David had asked her out, he promised to wine and dine her so that he could restore her faith in mankind and prove that not everyone she met was a Neanderthal dork – his words.

'How about changing the venue for that dinner?'

'That sounds very intriguing, where are you suggesting we dine Mr White?'

'Well, Ms White how about the upper deck of a 747?'

'A plane?'

'Not just any old plane, one which will drop us off in Barbados.'

'You're kidding?' Tanya gasped with delight.

'Do I seem to be the kidding kind? No, don't answer that...I have three weeks between now and when I have to get down to really hard graft, I won't have any other chance to get away. You, on the other hand are free and easy for the next couple of months, but I'd like to spend *my* three weeks with *you*.'

'And I would like nothing more than to spend it with you.' Tanya said softly. 'But I don't have any Barbados kind of clothes!'

'Me neither, we'll get some when we get there. I'll be at your parent's house at five-thirty to pick you up.'

'Hmm, it's a bit early for dinner, but, oh well, what the heck...Oh, Ok go on then, I suppose...seeing as you've gone to so much trouble, I can't refuse really, can I?'

'Erm...No.'

They both grinned as they put the phone down, amazed how life could turn itself upside down, on its head – before you even know what's happening.

One minute your life is in shreds and all about you is crumbling, then hey-bam! That proverbial new door opens... So, be warned!

6. The Story of Thomas Cotter
Chapter One

The clock, greeting him in the hallway, had stopped at 9:15. The smell of the house in Brighton had not changed in over four years. Carrots and hairspray.

When they had taken him away, that sunny summers evening in early August 1990, the police had insisted on placing handcuffs on him.

He had asked them why? Why did they have to humiliate him further?

They apologised and called him "*Sir*". Back at the yard, they spoke of him as a gentle man with more than seventy years of life behind him.

He had lived his life quietly, neatly. He had no fear of God, because he didn't believe in anything beyond the existence in which he lived. The things he endured during his marriage had stripped him of any faith, or joy, he had ever had or known.

Thomas was born in September 1919 - a product of the last days of the Great War - which made him ripe to fight for his King and country when World War II arrived in 1939.

Thomas had been courting Yvonne for only six months when he signed up, there had been no time to arrange a wedding before he was shipped out, but he bought her a ring and proposed - with the blessing of, at least, her family. Later, looking back on the situation, Thomas realised that her family had been putting subtle pressure on him, it had come along hand in hand with their smiles, whilst his parents tolerated it as they sat in the background of the exaggerated delight of her family.

'I promise you Yvonne, we will be wed the moment I come home,' he told her as he placed the small diamond ring onto her engagement finger.

'And I promise *you* Thomas Cotter, that should you return and not marry me, then your life will not be worth living.'

Thomas laughed aloud at her words, as did her mother and father. When Yvonne said such things to him he took them as cheekiness resulting from a feisty character. But more often than not, Yvonne didn't join in with his laughter; her words were delivered with the edge of a reapers sharpened scythe, and uttered in deadly seriousness which Thomas could not decipher.

He should have heeded his father's words: 'look at the mother, son…' he had told him on more than one occasion, 'that poor husband of hers is hen-pecked to an inch of his being.' Thomas poo-pooed his father's comment, he had found a girl to make him laugh and who seemed to be have been born with a natural wifely and home-making disposition. Love didn't come into it, he was totally enamoured by her and thought that it was natural that the care he felt would, in time, develop into love for his wife. Love he had grown up with, love as that which existed between his devoted parents. He had no doubt that she would make him a good wife and, in return, he would be a good and caring husband and father to their children.

****

Thomas was a good-looking lad with a face perpetually ready to break out with a grin and a smile; he was always on hand to help the neighbours with a few chores. He grew up in a two-up two-down; one of a string of houses in a terraced street in

Bermondsey, just off Southwark Park Road in South London, an area known to everyone as *Biscuit Town*. He was an only child and much loved. His father, like many of the men in their street, and some of the women too, worked at Peek Frean's biscuit factory on Drummond Road. The smell of baking biscuits filled the air and coated the washing as it dried, straddling the street as it hung between the houses. Thomas loved falling asleep in his soft bed, inhaling the soft smell of baking as he snuggled down, lost in a mountain of crisp sheets, wool blankets and satin eiderdown. It was the smell of his father and security.

Thomas couldn't wait to leave school and join his father at the factory; Peek, Frean & Co., they looked after their workers well, better than a lot of companies in those days. They even had doctors and dentists on site, they worked a pension fund and they even gave their employees a full week's pay and sent them home so they could go off on holiday.

His father still had the shrapnel of a bullet in his left leg, a memento of the Great War. He lived with the discomfort and walked with a limp and often, as he walked, his hand gripped the top of his leg until his knuckles turned white, this seemed to ease the tension and burning sensation surging through his leg. Many a night's sleep was broken when the pain burned deep. He kept the agony to himself; the things he had seen and lived through during those war-filled years, well, he never spoke of them. It wasn't the done thing, besides, no-one would really understand. Those years made his present life all the more joyous and precious. Each day with his wife and son was all he had dreamed of whilst he had laid low in the cold and damp, body-strewn trenches, filled with the stench of blood and faeces. Now, each new day his heart sprang alive with joy. He never took his life, nor his wife and son, for granted, he relished every moment spent with them, it was the best bonus a man could ever want.

He worked in the office at the factory, he went to work each day dressed in a three-piece woollen suit and tie, with his overcoat, or mac, buttoned up – the choice of coat depended on the season and the weather – he had several hats hanging on the pegs in the hallway; a homburg, a trilby and a couple of flat caps which Thomas would put on his head and saunter round the small house pretending he'd just returned home from work, it didn't last long, once his father saw him, he would repeat the same words he had the day before; "not in the house son, you don't wear your hat indoors." Another thing he taught his son was to always tip his hat when he was in the street and happened to come across someone he knew in passing. It was manners.

They had a fancy tin which his mother kept in the pantry, Thomas was allowed to open it after his tea and have one of the treats inside. He never knew what he would find in there; it depended on what bag of broken delicacies his dad brought home with him and what the factory had baked the day before – sweet or savoury?

Most days after school, and in the holidays, his mother had no idea where he was, she knew he would be somewhere in the street playing with the other kids, she had not a moments fear for his safety, the street was awash with surrogate mothers caring for each other's children.

Auntie Flo lived four doors down, she had been best friends with Thomas's mum since they were in the pram together. Auntie Flo had two children; Shirley, who was three months younger than Thomas, and Harold who was four years younger than the pair of them. Both mothers silently planned the marriage of Thomas and Shirley when they would be old enough to wed. To them, it was the natural way that life would flow and keep their families together.

Thomas left school at fifteen and the day after he joined his father as an employee of Peek Frean's. He took on a position working on the factory floor, he wore a white apron covering his clothes but still the flour covered him from head to toe. He would shake and beat his cap as soon as he got outside, the cloud of white flour would send a flutter of dust onto his already covered shoes.

He'd go into the alley at the back of the house and into the small yard, he'd knock on the scullery window to let his mum know he was home then he would go straight into the outside lavvie to change his clothes before he went indoors.

As he sat at the table with his father, eating their tea, they discussed their day at work and the things they had read in the paper, his mother would be out in the back yard hanging his clothes over the railing, she would beat them with the cane carpet beater, ready for him to wear the next day.

He knew that if he worked hard and showed his worth then he'd get promotion from the factory floor, he wanted to succeed and move on to work in the office like his father. He enjoyed the banter in the factory, even though you had to shout to be heard over the racket of the machines turning and hissing as the dough was pressed back and forth through the rollers, a giant version of his mother's wrought iron mangle which stood in the back yard.

The girls in the factory were all as pretty as a field of flowers, they wore their white uniforms which hid the fact that they were covered in a dusty layer of flour. Often a team was made up of three generations of women from the same family. Thomas had a twinkle in his eye as he teased the mothers and grandmothers, asking them if the *three sisters* were triplets and had they been in his class at school? His pretence of mock horror when they laughingly responded that they were old enough to be his mother and grandmother had the women giggling with endearment.

By the time Thomas had been at the factory for three years, he'd worked his way quite a way up from his original posting and, in the process of business, he expected his next step would be foreman, but the bosses thought otherwise: they offered him the position of a clerk in the office.

He was in two minds whether to take the offer or not. He talked it over with his father when they sat at the table having their tea that evening, the conversation continued as they sat in the easy chairs at the fireside. The father and son smoked their Woodbine cigarettes as his mother sat at the table darning her husband's socks.

'What do you think mum?' he turned to ask her.

'Well son, like your father says, it's a step in the right direction for you but, if as you say, you feel you want a bit more time on the factory floor then you need to speak your thoughts to them.'

His father threw his cigarette butt onto the coal fire, 'let me see these drawings you've been doing then.'

Thomas threw his cigarette butt into the embers and jumped up from his chair. Over the years at the factory he had become fascinated by the machinery, each working cog and turning handle had inspired engines and conveyor belts to be simplified in his mind. He had drawn illustrations to make the process work better. He went to get them to show his parents.

'I'm not saying that these will work or that it will make the system more productive but I have this feeling inside me that I can improve on the machinery we have now, I just need a bit more time working with them to see how I can achieve it.' Thomas said excitedly as he returned to the small room.

Thomas and his father joined his mother at the table where he opened his drawing book and explained the workings of his pencilled sketches. His mother had no idea if they were workable or not but she felt a huge surge of pride in her heart that her son was such a loveable, hard-working young lad and capable of making such a difference in life.

His father, having a knowledge of what he was talking about, studied the drawings for several minutes in silence.

'These are darn good my lad.'

Thomas beamed at his father's words. 'What do you think I should do dad?'

'Take these with you tomorrow and I'll arrange for you to have a meet-up with Mr Fraser, he's the man who keeps all the wheels and cogs moving. He'll be mighty impressed with these, I'm sure he will.'

The Story of Thomas Cotter
Chapter Two

Some would doubt that Yvonne Routledge had ever been young. As a child she was serious and smiles were a rarity, she took offence easily and twisted people's intentions into fabricated nastiness towards her, which she then returned with a cold stare and a haughty sniff. What she *was* good at, was manipulating people and hoodwinking them into believing she was a caring human being.

Some would say she got it from her mother, a woman who was known to begrudge the birds the air to fly. Her natural demeanour was to moan and complain about every insignificant and trivial matter, it was only when she wanted to impress someone would she then change her slant; then the smiles and the false words of kindness would flow, she would chat and exaggerate her family's standing in the community, all the while haughtily looking for some small sign to show her that this person she was talking to wasn't quite as elite as they made out.

They were a working class family, aspiring to a middle class lifestyle.

Both mother and daughter wore identical clothes, Yvonne was old before her time and spoke to her father in the same tone of voice she had heard her mother do all of her life.

Mr Routledge's wage was not enough to support the lifestyle Mrs Routledge had built up around her family and the day came when she told her daughter she would have to find some work to help pay the bills.

Yvonne was not only horrified but she was livid that she was expected to go out and toil to earn money. It was her mother who suggested she call upon the biscuit factory in

Bermondsey.

'Bermondsey?' Yvonne exclaimed in horror, 'that's the other side of the river, it will take me more than an hour to get there each day, and then there's my return journey. Anyway mother, if I must go out to work then so should you!'

Her mother ignored her comment.

Yvonne's mother did not want her working close to home, people would talk and she hated the thought of them saying that her daughter was a mere factory girl.

****

The first thing Yvonne did the day she started at Peek Frean's in Bermondsey was to look for a suitable husband to get her out of this whole mess of having to work.

It was just before she was due to go on her tea-break at 10:30 when she spied him, he walked down the aisle in his woollen three-piece suit and a pair of very fine leather shoes, Yvonne knew that these were from *Crockett & Jones* the shoemaker, an advert for the very same pair had been cut out of the newspaper by her mother and placed in the scrapbook she kept of: *The most desirable things one can possess*. She made a mental note to check the price of the shoes when she returned home that evening.

Yvonne noticed how all the girls, and even the older ladies, sprang to life as he came whistling by. He stopped here and there to have a quick chat with one or two of them. His face was friendly and his smile caused the creases around his eyes to explode like a shattering of stars.

'Who is that?' Yvonne asked Stella, the young girl working by her side.

'Ah, that's our Thomas Cotter. The nicest fella you could

ever meet.' Stella smiled as she noticed the look on Yvonne's face, 'and no, he ain't courting, but there's more than a dozen lasses here would jump at the chance if he asked them. He used to be on the factory floor here,' she carried on telling Yvonne the story, 'but a couple of months ago he got promoted up to the office, he's a genius at all the engineering stuff, some say that he's drawing up plans to get all the factory updated with his custom made machines.'

'Clever then, is he?'

'Not 'alf! He'll go far, that one will.'

Unbeknown to him, those words sealed Thomas Cotter's destiny.

****

He came down at the oddest of times, Yvonne felt slightly peeved at his irregular timing, there was no telling what time he'd be in her aisle to have a chat and to have a flirt with the girls; that annoyed her too, it would need to stop once they were betrothed, she wouldn't put up with such behaviour.

'Are you going to go for your tea-break?' Stella asked her. 'It's nearly half past.'

Yvonne didn't want to leave her post. 'We can swap if you wish?' she said kindly.

'But you're not feeling well…'

Yvonne had told her colleague that she felt she was getting sick, that she hadn't slept well – this was part of her plan.

'Oh, don't worry about me, you've been up half the night with your little one. Go on, you go and have a nice cup of tea and a biscuit or two, that'll put you on your feet again. I'm just feeling a bit off colour that's all, I'll be fine, go on…'

'Are you sure?' her colleague turned, ready to go, 'you are

such a lovely work mate, thank you.'

'Oh, I wouldn't say that,' Yvonne smiled falsely and urged Stella mentally to get a move on; she could see him coming down the aisle, getting closer.

It would take him a couple of minutes until he passed her, up until now he'd done no more than nod his head and give her a smile, today would be different, it would all be in her timing. Unlike him, Yvonne knew the precision of seconds and how they could affect the moment - and the future.

Out of the side of her eye she could see him getting closer, she clutched the side of the tray she was unloading the biscuits from, she breathed heavily in and out and then, when he was nearly upon her she began to crumple, her knees buckled and she hung onto the side of the table until Thomas grabbed her, held her up, close to his body. She leaned against him as his arms enfolded her securely.

Thomas called out loud for someone to get the doctor.

'Oh, please, I'm fine. Really, I'm fine.' Yvonne strained her eyes to roll upwards, feigning virtual loss of consciousness

'Good lord girl, you're not fine at all.' Thomas looked around trying to see if the doctor, or at least the nurse, was on the way. 'What's your name?' he asked, worried that she may pass out; he wanted to keep her awake and talking.

'Yvonne,' she told him with a sigh as she rested her head against his shoulder.

'Oh, very posh!' He smiled at her, trying to lighten the moment and the panic he felt. He'd never held a woman in this way before, her body felt nice next to his, he squeezed his arms closer around her.

'It's French.' She allowed her knees to give way so that he

had to hold her up again.

'Where's that help? For crying out loud this girl is sick…'

Yvonne signed off work for two days; she took to her bed at home and remained there, she expelled a constant stream of demands on her mother who grumbled as she waited on her daughter hand and foot.

On Thursday she returned to her station in the factory. Stella had been worried and felt guilty that she had taken the tea-break in her place. She let everyone know what a selfless, kind and sweet young woman Yvonne was.

Those words reached Thomas' ears; he remembered the feel of her in his arms and he couldn't stop thinking about her.

He knew that both his mum and dad, and Auntie Flo, had high hopes for him and Shirley to wed but it wouldn't happen. The pair of them were as close as siblings and it was beyond anything they would ever dream of happening, it just wasn't right, no matter which way they looked at it. Anyway, Shirley had her eye on one of the lads Thomas played cricket with, so he had taken her with him, to every game. He introduced her to Bertie as his non-related-sister and when they became a couple Thomas told Bertie that if he ever hurt Shirley, then he would have him to deal with.

Yvonne saw him coming down the wooden staircase at the far end of the factory.

'I say my love, would you mind if I go off for my tea-break a few moments early?' Yvonne asked Stella who was still consumed with guilt.

'No, of course not. Are you feeling unwell?'

'I'm fine, honestly,' Yvonne patted the woman's arm, 'a cup of sweet tea will perk me up.'

'Go! Go now and take as long as you want. I don't need a break today, really I don't, so don't hurry back.'

Yvonne smiled with a look of effort on her face, 'you really are the dearest colleague I could ever wish for.'

She walked down the aisle with her head bent, pretending not to see him walking towards her.

'Yvonne!' He said her name with such relief in his voice.

She raised her eyes from the floor and looked at him quizzically, as if she didn't recognise him.

'It's Thomas, I was the one who came to your aid…'

'Oh! I'm glad to see you again,' she said in a tone her mother would have used, 'I wanted to find you, to thank you for your help the other day, when I was taken ill.'

'No thanks needed. Are you well again? I came down each day to see if you had returned.'

'Did you Thomas? How very sweet of you.'

Thomas blushed and tried to hide a smile.

'I'm just on my way for my tea-break. If you have no immediate work to complete, perhaps you would join me?' When Yvonne wanted something she would fight for it and let nothing stand in her way.

Thomas blushed even more as he remembered the feeling which rushed through his body when he held her close to him, a few days ago, 'yes, yes, I can take a break.'

****

It didn't take long for him to become smitten with the vixen. Yvonne would let her charade slip but Thomas didn't notice the different character coming through, she would snap at him and tut disapprovingly when he made jovial comments. He actually thought it was rather sweet and all part of her caring nature.

One day they were walking arm in arm along his street, the neighbour a few doors down was on her hands and knees scrubbing the front step. Her upper body swung from side to side, quickly with the motion of the scrubbing brush, her large round bottom, on the other hand, moved in the opposite direction – just as briskly.

Thomas loved to see this, sometimes he would look up or down the street and there'd be half a dozen bottoms swinging away, it always made him laugh and goodness knows how many times he wanted to run down the street and slap each bottom as he ran past - all in good fun, of course.

As they got closer to his neighbour, Thomas reached up to tip his hat to greet her, 'good evening Mrs B, you're looking as lovely as ever I see.' Thomas winked and gave her a wide smile.

'Ooh…' she laughed as she pulled herself up, 'you're full of it you are. You need to keep your eye on that one Yvonne.' Mrs B said jokingly.

Out of ear shot Yvonne took her arm out of his, 'why do you have to do that?' she asked him in an unreasonable tone.

Thomas didn't understand what the problem was, 'what do you mean? Do What?'

'It is so disrespectful to philander with that woman.'

Thomas laughed nervously, 'I've known her all my life, she's old enough to be my grandmother, I always tease her, it means nothing. She feels no disrespect in the slightest!'

'Not her – me! That was so disrespectful to *me*, how do you think I feel when you talk to another woman like that? How would you like it if I spoke to other men in the way you do these women?'

'Well, I suppose…'

'Exactly, now please have some thought for me.'

'I'm sorry Yvonne, really I am. You know that you're the only girl for me, don't you?' He pulled her into the back alley and stroked her hair. She'd promised him that this evening he could put his hand inside her bra again; she would allow him to knead her warm breast. If he upset her now she may change her mind, he couldn't bear it, he'd thought of nothing else all day. 'You know that no-one can turn my head from you.' Slowly, he moved his hand closer to her left breast, 'your heart is beneath here,' he pressed his hand through her clothing, 'and that heart beats for me, just as mine beats for you.' He pulled her closer and kissed her neck, his hand squeezed her buttock and pulled her closer to his rigid penis.

Yvonne pulled herself away coyly, 'oh Thomas, you know that we can't do *that*, not until we are married.'

'Do what?' he laughed, knowing that she would tease and please him.

'This,' her hand moved slowly down between their bodies and her fingers softly stroked the length of his erect penis through his clothes. '*But*, if you promise never to speak or humiliate me again in front of other women, I may let you kiss my breast, later.'

Thomas gasped, she had never allowed him to kiss her breast before, he longed to feel her hard nipple between his lips.

'I promise and I swear my darling Yvonne, that I will never speak to another women in such a way again.'

'You need to curb your chatty ways with the women and girls at the factory too, it doesn't look right…now that you and me are together, a real couple.' He would promise her anything, for the feel of her breast against his lips, his face.

The Story of Thomas Cotter
Chapter Three

Early in 1939 both Britain and France warned Germany that they would not stand by and watch if their threat to invade Poland materialised. When, early in September that same year, Germany took no notice and marched its army into Poland, World War II began. No-one could know the outcome or the destruction and loss of life it would create. No-one was untouched, as the world wept.

The seeds for this war had been sown by the Treaty of Versailles that ended World War I. Hitler went ahead anyway, fully understanding the consequences.

Thomas and Bertie went in to London town and signed up. The managers at Peek, Frean & Co., told Thomas that his job would be waiting for his return.

Yvonne thought he would be better suited to a desk job in Whitehall but she felt this was one situation she would lose her argument with, and so, she told him she would let him go to war and the day he returned she would be waiting in her wedding gown.

The letters from home kept them all going, just a few words from their loved ones gave them more spirit than anyone back home could have imagined. Parcels from the Red Cross at Christmas had Thomas laughing heartily, he opened his box to find a tin of *Peek Frean's Christmas Pudding*. How he longed to be back there, the sweet smell of biscuits filling the air, the washing hung across the street flapping in the wind, the fat bottomed ladies swinging from side to side as they scrubbed their front steps. His mum and dad; what he would give to sit at the tea table, laughing and talking as they used to.

And the warmth of Yvonne's breast against his face, they'd get married as soon as he was home, he'd go back to the factory and pick up where he left off – it was a good wage and they'd be able to buy themselves a little house close by. It was beyond words just how much he missed his community and he longed for the day when he would be back with them.

After nearly six years of fighting throughout the world, and the killing of nearly 60 million people across the globe, the war was finally over.

It was a phrase which could be heard through every dale and valley throughout the land; as loved ones returned home they told their family and neighbours that *they* were *the lucky ones*.

****

Whether it was the war which had drained his emotions, or the fatigue which racked his body, Thomas felt half-hearted on his wedding day, he would have been happy to delay it by a few months so that he could stay at home with his parents, amongst those he knew and felt at ease with, but Yvonne had it all planned.

Once they were married they moved into her parent's house in the East End, he felt as though he'd lost a limb. But it was only temporary, this he kept telling himself as he sat each evening listening to the two women berate his poor father-in-law, and their crude words describing their next door neighbour's choice of curtains.

It would be different once they had a place of their own, he told himself. Yvonne had said that once they had saved a bit more they could try for a family and get a decent house, until such a time they would live with her parents.

Sunday, the 2nd of January 1949, and they were still living with the in-laws. Yvonne was heavily pregnant with their first child which was due the following week.

Sunday was the day Thomas looked forward to as this was the day they would go to Bermondsey to spend time, have lunch with his parents. Today though, Yvonne said she was too tired, it would be too much for her, she said. He should go alone but be sure to be home by six o'clock.

A flutter of relief escaped inside his stomach as he put on his overcoat and tucked his scarf neatly across his chest. He dreamed constantly of the day they had saved enough for a house in Bermondsey. It was the dream which kept him going.

Thomas took home a good wage each week, he handed the £5 he earned over to his wife, she took care of the money. When he asked if they had enough to buy all the furniture she wanted for their new house, she would tell him, "no, not yet."

He crossed Tower Bridge and the smell was like a cloud drifting closer to him, this was what he looked forward to each day as he arrived, south of the river, on his way to work. The smell of sweet baking enticing him closer and closer, until he felt he was home, again.

Thomas rattled his knuckles on the glass pane of the scullery to let his parents know he was home. He went in to the warm room with the fire blazing, his easy chair by the fireside waiting for him.

'I'm on my own today mum,' he told his mother as he hugged her tight and kissed her soft cheek.

'Oh, well, never mind. I expect Yvonne wants a bit of a rest, what with her being so close to her time.' Ellen Cotter was rather pleased, she had her son to herself for once. When Yvonne came with him she felt she was under her constant scrutiny. Even when she hugged her own child or ruffled his hair as he sat at the table she could sense Yvonne shudder with displeasure. It didn't bother her, nothing or no-one could take her son and his love away from her, and she would never stop showering the affection she had on him, she was secure in that. But, it was seeing him hold his tongue, how his spontaneous laughter and cheekiness had been snatched away from his natural disposition, it was this which made her so very cross with his wife.

'I love being home mum.' Thomas told his mother as she stirred the meat stock ready for the gravy. They still had rations but there was always ways to get things and neighbours living in Biscuit Town always knew someone who made sure that they didn't go without.

'And I love you being here Thomas,' she turned and squeezed his cheek. 'If only we had another bedroom, then you could live here, with us…' His mother sighed inwardly.

Yvonne had said that it was impossible to live in that small house, at least her parent's house had more rooms and space.

'Let's hope it won't be long till we've got enough money together to get a place of our own, over on this side.'

'We've told you, me and your dad have a bit put away. We can help…'

'I know mum, but you and dad should spend it on yourselves, that's your money. I'm earning a good wage so it shouldn't be long now.'

'What do me and your dad need? We've got everything we could ever want.'

'You could buy yourselves a little car, take yourselves off to the coast now and then.'

His mother laughed, 'I don't think so, but if *you* wanted a car…'

'NO, mum!' He laughed with her, 'anyway, where's dad?' he asked as he walked into the living room.

'He's just popped up to see old Mr Mitchell, his toilet chain's broken and the poor old soul couldn't flush, he'll be back in a minute.'

At five o'clock Thomas put on his coat and scarf ready to go home, if only he could stay…his heart was heavy but it was his duty to return to his wife on the other side of the river.

'I'll see you in the morning dad,' Thomas patted his father's shoulder as he walked towards his mother. 'I'll see you on Wednesday.' He opened his arms to hug her tight.

'Take care my love and I'll see you for your dinner on Wednesday.'

Twice a week Thomas would leave the factory at mid-day sharp and walk home with his father for lunch. Wednesday was always meat pie. His mother made the best meat pie he had ever tasted, they had it with mashed potato and cabbage. The pastry of her pie was crispy on the edges and soft with suet inside.

His father would sprinkle his dinner with pepper; the smell would reach Thomas' nostrils – another scent to fill him with the comfort and love of home.

On a Wednesday they were allowed a longer dinner-time, they didn't need to be back at work until three o'clock. Father and son would stroll back to the office, past the shops which were all closed on a Wednesday afternoon, it was their time together to discuss the goings on in the world.

On a Friday, dinner was fish and chips. No chippie *anywhere* made a better batter than the one his mum made.

Thomas set off into the cold dark evening, his heart kept buoyant by the thought of the birth of his child, by this time next week, he thought to himself, he could be a father. Hopefully, Yvonne would then see that they needed a home of their own.

He had no idea how much money they had saved, he would ask her when he got home, he would put his foot down, for surely, he made a quick mental calculation, they should have at least £400 saved by now. He knew that Yvonne gave her mother rent and food money for their keep, which was natural, but that shouldn't have been more than two guineas a week.

No, he had had enough living under their roof, it was time for them to move on.

****

He didn't expect a warm greeting when he got back to his in-laws, he never did, but the cold stare from his mother-in-law made him stand still with shock.

'Typical!' she hissed as he unbuttoned his thick coat, 'where were you when your wife needed you? Oh, down the pub with your father I suppose!'

'What's the matter? What's happened?' He hung his coat up on the peg which had been allocated to him on the inside of the cupboard door. 'Where's Yvonne?'

'Oh, now you're worried about your wife are you? Well you should have been here three hours ago when she suffered the pain of giving birth to your daughter.'

Thomas ignored the sour tone to her words, his face lit up. 'Daughter? I have a daughter?' The joy in his heart exploded with love, he ran towards the stairs.

'You can't go up there!' Mrs Routledge scoffed angrily.

113

Thomas stopped, 'why?' he feared something was wrong with his child.

'Take your dirty shoes off, I don't want mud all over the stair carpet. I'm the one who'd be on my hands and knees cleaning it off…'

Thomas hastily untied the laces and kicked off his shoes, he left them in the hallway; sod what the old bat thought, he didn't hear her protestations that he shouldn't walk around in his stocking feet, he left her voice behind as he ran up the stairs two at a time.

The baby was wrapped tightly in a blanket in a crib by the side of the bed. Yvonne was asleep, her mouth was wide open and a grating noise came from the back of her throat.

Mrs Routledge followed him upstairs.

'Don't go waking the pair of them.' She pushed by him, blocking his view of his sleeping child. 'Barbara didn't stop crying for the first two hours.'

'Barbara?'

'Your daughter!'

'That wasn't a name we ever discussed. If we had a boy we decided to call him Michael and Helen for a girl.' He had managed to persuade his wife that Helen was a glamorous name, he would shorten it, in time, to Ellen – after his beloved mother.

'Such common names,' she tutted, 'Barbara is better.'

Thomas sat on the edge of the bed and watched his child sleeping, her little mouth opening in a yawn, she flapped one arm in the air. He reached inside the crib and placed his finger in the palm of her tiny hand, she gripped it tightly and twisted her head around in her sleep. Thomas felt tears stinging his eyes, he longed to pick her up and kiss her sweet scented forehead, but his mother in law hovered over him like a prison warden.

'I've made up the bed in the small box room for you for tonight,' she told him.

'What? Why?'

'You men haven't the sense you were born with…Yvonne needs to have her rest and she'll be much better on her own than having a big snoring lout lying next to her.'

Thomas left for work the next morning without yet even held his daughter. He left the house an hour earlier than normal, he wanted to call in on his mother before work, to tell her the news.

The Story of Thomas Cotter
Chapter Four

In 1952, Yvonne decided they had enough saved to move to their own home. Thomas had all but given up hope of them ever leaving the depressing house in East London. He knew that he would have a battle on his hands, persuading her that Bermondsey was the better place to be, it wouldn't be easy, but as he was working longer hours and had more responsibility in the engineering department, he would tell her that it would be better for them to live closer to the factory.

Yvonne had different ideas. She knew her husband wanted to return to his old home ground but that was the last place she wanted to be. She despised his friendship with his old childhood friend Shirley. Even though she was now married to Bertie, Yvonne felt a jealous anger twist inside her gut whenever her name was mentioned.

His parents left her feeling unworthy of their son, his mother treated him like a child, she smothered him in love, for goodness sake he was a grown man with a family of his own and he should start to leave his old life behind him.

No, Yvonne had other ideas and she would make sure she got her way.

Barbara was proving to be a difficult child, she cried and threw tantrums which would last for an hour or more. When he was there, Thomas would pick her up and hold her close, he would try and distract her with songs and nursery rhymes or a cat climbing the tree in the front garden. She would be soothed for a few seconds but then her legs and hands would kick out at her father and he had to put her back down again. It broke his heart that he couldn't reach her but he truly believed that she acted in such a way because she was intelligent and she felt frustrated that the words in her head could not be spoken out loud. Once she started school and her intelligence could find itself, she would be better.

It was early spring when he came home from work one evening and Yvonne was abnormally happy. She greeted him in the hall and took his mac to hang up, she was smiling as she told him that she had had the most wonderful day.

'Mother and father are selling this old house!' She squeezed her husband's hand and continued to smile.

Thomas grinned too. 'That's wonderful news! It means we will have no choice but to find a home of our own,' he pulled his wife close to him and held her close, he couldn't remember the last time he had felt her body this close to him. 'We could even think of trying for another baby, a brother or sister for Babs?'

'Barbara.' His wife corrected him. 'No, that is a dreadful idea. Barbara needs good clean air and space to run, she doesn't need another little person taking the attention away from her, besides, you seem to forget that it is *I* who will be the one to suffer because of your selfishness.'

Thomas pulled away from her, she had the ability to dehydrate his heart in one sentence.

'I know the best place for us to live.'

'Oh, you do? Where's that then?' A hint of sarcasm tinged his voice, disappointment riddled his veins before she had even told him her idea.

'Brighton. And before you say anything, I have been reading about it in a magazine. We can get a lot more house for our money than we can here in London. Mother and father have found a perfect little bungalow for themselves, with views of the sea for a fraction of the price of this house.'

The picture danced in his head of her parents living close by and he being cut-off from those he truly loved.

'What about my work?'

'You are worth much more than a silly biscuit factory Thomas, you need to exert yourself more.'

'I have a very good job here…'

'Yes, and you could do better. If you take your weekly holiday – you can tell them tomorrow you need to plan your time off – the five of us shall spend a week in Brighton, by the sea, and we shall find our new home.'

****

The day Thomas walked out of Peek, Frean & Co. for the last time, his heart broke into a thousand pieces. The whole factory stood waving their white flour-dusty cloths, they sang *We'll Meet Again* as he walked down each aisle of the factory bidding his farewells. Both men and women reached out and gripped his hand, they told him they would miss him. Some of the women cried as they wished him well and told him they would never forget him.

Thomas found work easy enough in Brighton. The hours were longer, the pay was less, the people weren't as friendly but it was close enough to their new house and he could cycle to work each day. He spent his lunchtime eating his sandwiches and reading the newspaper in the park behind his office.

Often, he would return home after his day at work to find his mother-in-law sat in his favourite chair, she would stay there, parked and unmoveable for the next three or four hours.

Yvonne made decisions without him, she took his wage packet each week and gave him a couple of shillings from it, she expected him to save this to buy gifts for her birthday and Christmas.

They'd been in Brighton for nearly a year when Thomas arrived home one evening in early winter to find his wife sat in the hallway on a piece of furniture she had bought a few weeks previously; she was talking on a telephone. A telephone that had not been in his house when he left home that morning, nor had he been given any inkling that such a thing was about to arrive.

Once she had finished her lengthy discussion, she laughed, pleased with herself, and took a bright yellow duster out of the drawer of the telephone table, she polished the cream, ivory coloured receiver before placing the handset down on the cradle.

'Well, my word.' Thomas looked at the phone and had no idea why they needed such a thing; they didn't know anyone else who had one.

'You can't be surprised, surely?' Yvonne scoffed at him as she flicked the duster over the wooden piece of furniture. 'I told you this was a telephone table when I bought it the other week.'

'No, actually, you told me it was a hallway table.'

Yvonne glared at him, 'I know what I told you Thomas, if you choose not to listen to your wife's conversation then I'm afraid you need to become a better husband.'

It wasn't worth Thomas getting in to an argument. 'Who were you talking to on the phone?'

'Mother, she has the same model and the same table.'

'Your mother lives a five minute walk away, you see her every day, why do you need to talk to her on the telephone?'

'I'm not going to explain myself to you Thomas, you

wouldn't understand.'

'Probably not,' he muttered to himself as he hung up his coat and took of his shoes. He pushed his feet inside his slippers and he realised that if he got his parents to get a telephone he would be able to speak to them regularly. He knew how to use a phone, from the one's in the office. A couple of times he had even phoned his father at the factory, for a quick chat, it always lightened his day.

'What's our number?' He asked her, he would phone his father tomorrow and tell him their number and ask him to arrange a phone for home.

'Why would you want the number?' Yvonne polished the handle on the cupboard door which Thomas had just closed.

'In case I have an emergency at work, I can call you.'

Yvonne pointed to the dial on the phone, the number was written in the middle.

A few weeks later he arrived home and found his easy chair had been moved to accommodate a three-tier, gilt, four-wheeled tea trolley. The tiers were mock-marble edged in a balcony of gilt.

A few days later the top tier of the tea trolley had been filled with a set of rose-patterned porcelain tea cups and saucers, small plates and silver cake forks. The trolley had been covered with a plastic tent and he was warned not to touch it, Barbara had been threatened with no more sugar sandwiches if she ever went near it.

He didn't notice when a matching cake stand took its place in the middle of the cups and saucers, under the plastic canopy.

To most people such a life would be intolerable but Thomas felt his responsibility as a father and husband had been set in stone, and it was his duty to ensure they were cared for. He escaped the dreariness by reminiscing in his head of his life in Bermondsey, and he became lost in the books he borrowed from the local library.

****

By the time Barbara was ready for secondary school it became apparent to everyone that she was a child with demons in her soul. She would hit out at her father for no reason, Yvonne blamed him for being so soft with her when she was a baby and a toddler, he had ruined her. Thomas knew that it was something far deeper than that. One of his colleagues at work spoke about his own daughter who had problems with her behaviour, she had been taken into care where she was being looked after with specialised help. It hadn't been an easy decision, he told Thomas, but it was not safe for her to live in the house.

One night, his colleague told him, he had woken to the smell of burning, he woke his wife and told her to get out of the house with their daughter. He ran downstairs to find a pan on kitchen stove with flames jumping around it. His daughter had gone down to make herself a fried egg but she had left it and gone back to bed.

Thomas knew that Barbara was not a danger in that sense but he asked his colleague if he thought he should speak to the doctor about his daughter. His colleague told him that he believed he should.

He tried to reason with Yvonne that it was in Barbara's best interest to get help for the poor girl, as she matured it would only get worse if they didn't seek help.

'My daughter is not a lunatic. How dare you go behind my

back and gossip in such a cruel way to a stranger?' she spat at her husband, 'goodness knows *who* he will now go and tell. I can't go out now can I? I will hear every stuck up nose whispering behind my back; *there goes that woman with a lunatic for a daughter.*'

Thomas wasn't a weak man but he had no words, nor heart, for such a conversation with his wife so he let it go, he let her win the battle.

****

In 1959 Yvonne decided they should buy a car, she chose a cream Ford Anglia which had a baby-blue coloured roof and a flash of a stripe along the side. Thomas had his driving licence from his days in the army. Yvonne didn't wish to learn to drive.

Thomas returned to Bermondsey to visit his parents once a month, he went alone which secretly pleased not only him but his parents as well. The drive home always thrilled him, he still dreamed that, one day, life would return to the good days that he had known, it was a dream which kept him going.

By the mid-sixties it became clear that Barbara needed that specialist care which Thomas had tried to persuade his wife, a few years before. This time, Yvonne allowed Thomas to contact the doctor recommended by his colleague. It was agreed that Barbara would now live in the home fifteen miles outside of Brighton and she would go home to her parents every other weekend.

Yvonne told everyone that her daughter was ill from exhaustion and that she was staying with friends who had a large estate in the country.

The house was quiet without their daughter. His wife would spend her evenings talking on the phone to her mother, only replacing the receiver when it was time for Emergency Ward 10 or Coronation Street.

The gilt and marble-effect tea trolley still sat in the corner next to his chair, unused and with its plastic tent which his wife dusted each day.

Yvonne's mother died suddenly in 1971, she died in her sleep. Unbeknown to any of them she had become diabetic, in her sleep she had drifted into a coma from which she never awoke. Yvonne was beside herself with grief and blamed her father for not realising her mother had been ill, if he had not been sleeping in the spare room he would have woken when she needed help.

They tried to explain to her that it happened as she slept, she did not wake and her father was not to blame. Yvonne thought differently and never let him forget it.

Two years later, without telling her, her father sold up and moved along the coast to Worthing. They didn't keep in contact and Yvonne never heard from her father again.

According to her, he was acting true to form – the thoughtless, uncaring person that he was.

In 1978 Thomas was made a partner of his firm, they called him The Engineer and he was the first person they went to with their problems. He was a good listener too and everyone knew that if you had a problem then speaking to Thomas always helped and he never broke your confidence, he kept your troubles to himself.

****

Recently, Thomas noticed, his mum's mind seemed to drift off when he was talking to her, in the middle of their conversation she would start talking about someone they knew years before. His father told him that she'd gone to bake a cake and put it the bathroom cupboard instead of the oven. They'd laughed about it, not realising that it was the beginning of her dementia.

A few years before, the council had moved everyone from the terrace street into flats they had specially built a spit and a throw away. His mum and dad had been given a ground floor flat, due to his father's leg which had become more painful and troublesome and he found it difficult to climb stairs. They had a small garden and most of their old neighbours were still close by. The community spirit still lived on.

Late November 1980 Thomas got a late night call from his father to say that his mum had been taken into hospital. She was completely disorientated and he had to call the doctor out, he was beside himself with worry. Thomas backed the Volvo out of the garage and told his wife he would call her later. He drove to London, fearful of seeing his beloved mother in a state of distress.

The doctors discovered that his mother had fractured her hip, it wasn't something which had happened recently as it had healed over but it was disjointed and would be causing her great pain.

They knew that she had pain in her hip; she walked with a limp and she couldn't place her left foot flat on the ground, she would only sit in a dining chair as getting up from the settee or easy chair was too painful for her. Whenever they mentioned it and told her to go to the doctor she always replied that it was the aches and pains of old age and the doctors could do nothing. During the last couple of years she would rub balm onto the painful joint, the smell of camphor and cloves was always strong in their flat.

His father's leg, still with shrapnel from the war, was causing him more pain and he also found it difficult to walk. Neither of them ever complained, they still smiled and their faces lit up when their son walked in.

They had never spent a night apart; they still slept together in the same bed as they had done every night for the last sixty-odd years. With his wife in hospital, Harold Cotter told his son that he would go to the doctor, his leg was getting bad, his circulation wasn't working as it should and his toes, foot and ankle were turning black.

Before going to visit his mother the next day, he took his father to the doctor. The doctor sent him to hospital immediately; gangrene had taken over and his leg was seriously infected.

They operated and removed his left leg that same day.

Thomas went to visit his mother, he didn't tell her that his father was in hospital too, or that he'd had an operation to remove his leg. He wasn't sure whether she would have understood. She was still the wonderful sweet woman he loved beyond words. She told him stories of when he was little, she laughed and her eyes watered with her laughter. She told him how handsome his father was, how she fell in love with him the first time she saw him. But she didn't ask where he was or why he hadn't been to visit her.

Thomas returned to his father's bedside in London Bridge Hospital – all paid for by his pension fund from Peek Frean's –

and told him how his mother was still the warm and lovely woman they both knew and loved.

His father laughed softly and said, 'you know son, I think I've had enough now. I've had my time, I'm ready to go.'

Thomas knew what he was saying, he was at the end of his life.

'I couldn't have wanted for a better lad than you, we had a right good old time, didn't we? The three of us?'

Thomas laughed softly, he felt the ache in his throat trying to hold back the tears which wanted to creep out, he knew he didn't have much time left with his father.

'I would have liked more for you. I know not every man is blessed with having a wife as wonderful as your mother, or having a life full of love – like we have. But I would have liked more for you son.' His words were not said with any acrimony. 'I've never believed in God, you know that, but I reckon I was wrong. I wish I'd given it more thought, there's something there, I can feel it and…it's amazing. Don't give up son.'

Harold Cotter smiled as he sighed and closed his eyes, he gripped his son's hand one last time before he went.

The following day Thomas drove across London to the small hospital to visit his mother, he wouldn't tell her that her husband passed away last night. It probably wouldn't register with her and, even if it did, it would cause her undue distress. He knew that his mother would never leave hospital. They would move her to a home where she would be cared for, he would tell her in good time.

Ellen Cotter was sat in a chair by her bed watching a couple of squirrels darting around on the lawn outside. Someone had combed her hair, they hadn't done it right.

'Hello mum,' Thomas bent to kiss her, her face beamed a smile of recognition, she reached up to stroke his face, her other hand held her hankie tightly inside her curled fingers. Thomas inhaled the camphor and cloves, she had an aura of beauty, like a halo, surrounding her.

'Are you staying long?' She asked him.

Thomas reached into the locker for her brush and comb, he stood up and combed her hair into the style it should be, 'there, that's better. You look like my mum again.'

'Oooo,' she inhaled and rubbed his hand, 'you are such a lovely lad. Your dad and I were saying the self-same thing last night.'

'Dad?' Thomas held her clenched hand.

'Yes, he came to see me. He's coming back soon, he's coming for me.'

Thomas knew that he needn't have worried about telling her his father had died, he should have known that their bond was too intense for her not to know, that his father would never leave her on her own.

Two days later Ellen Cotter died peacefully in her sleep.

The turn-out for their funeral was overwhelming, all the old colleagues from the factory, neighbours and dear friends, they laughed and they cried, they told stories which Thomas had never heard before which made him laugh out loud. Everyone said the same; they had to go together, it was a natural thing for they couldn't have lived a day without each other in the same world.

Thomas' parents were cremated, their ashes together in the urn, side by side, never to be parted again.

****

Thomas's life revolved around his work, his books, visiting his daughter one weekend and caring for her the other. He had become adept at building a wall of steel around him when his wife was in the vicinity.

Tomorrow was just something which followed the night of today and would be coped with as, and when, it arrived.

1990, Thomas was still a partner at the engineering firm but he didn't go in to the office every day. He didn't want to stop work altogether, and his wife had told him that she wouldn't put up with him in the house all day long, getting under her feet and making a mess every time he moved.

On the days when he didn't go to the office he visited his daughter and helped out in the kitchen, he chopped vegetables and washed the pans. He didn't tell Yvonne that this is where he went to get out from under her feet, she wasn't bothered where he went as long as he kept away until six o'clock each evening, this was the routine she was used to and she couldn't cope with anything else.

'Where do you go when you're not at work?' she once asked him with a look of disgust on her face.

'I do a bit of voluntary work,' he answered honestly, 'why?'

'You smell of old cabbage whenever you come home, can you go and get a wash please.' She huffed again. 'It's not with those homeless people is it? Please, don't tell me you're mixing with tramps, I'll have to disinfect your clothes…'

'No Yvonne.'

Next time she went to her women's meeting she bragged how her husband was involved with a charity and worked voluntarily for its good cause. When they asked her which charity it was, she told them she didn't want to say as it would seem as though she were bragging.

August 1990 was hot, so hot that a new record was set. There was no reprise from the heat, roads melted and fights broke out in supermarkets as people became fraught with the heat, they grappled over the last ice creams in the freezers and people drowned trying to cool off in pools. At least on the coast they had the sea to keep the temperature slightly down from that in London.

Thomas paid a visit to a company he had dealt with for many years, he knew they would have a solution to help him sleep better, the nights were sweltering hot and made sleep impossible.

The small fans made no impact, he needed something more robust so, early in the afternoon of Thursday 9th August 1990, Thomas drove to R.T. Roberts and picked up two mobile air conditioning units. He knew that if he didn't get two then he would have to go without, Yvonne would demand it for her room.

'They can be a bit noisy so I've put a bag of ear plugs in there for you.' Ronald Roberts told him.

'They'll come in handy when the wife gets a bit chatty!' Thomas laughed, playing along as he always did, never letting anyone know of the relentless nagging of his wife.

He pulled up in the driveway and unloaded the first unit, he took it in through the front door so he could get it upstairs easier.

'What do you think you're doing?' Yvonne had come into the hallway, she didn't like him using the front door, he should use the back.

'I need to get this air conditioning unit upstairs; at least it'll give me a decent night's sleep.'

'It will give *you* a decent night's sleep?' Yvonne snarled, 'what a selfish man you are,' she sneered and curled her top lip.

Thomas was in no mood to explain that he had two units, his temper was starting to fray. He left the unit in the middle of the hallway and went to the kitchen for a glass of water.

Yvonne followed him, berating him for his lack of compassion to her needs.

He drank his water at the sink, her words were just a sound, like tinnitus in his head. He squeezed his eyes tight trying to get rid of the buzzing.

He washed the glass he had used and dried it with the tea towel before returning it to the cupboard.

Yvonne opened the cupboard telling him that he had placed the glass on the wrong shelf.

'*This* is a tall glass which belongs on the top shelf!' she was shouting at him as though he were a child, 'upside down on the tea towel, you stupid man.' She put the glass in place herself and turned to carry on her nagging.

'Oh shut up woman, shut up!' he yelled at her, never before in his life had he raised his voice, to anyone, let alone his insufferable spouse.

The kettle was in his hand, he had no recollection of picking it up, he swung round and hit her on the side of her head. Her body flew across the kitchen where she hit the other side of her head on the corner of the work surface.

Thomas stood with the kettle still in his hand, his was gasping for breath as he looked at her lying on the floor. He felt no fear for his actions as he went to her, he was still gasping for air as he turned her body over, her eyes were open. She was dead.

Thomas Cotter was charged with manslaughter and sentenced to five years in prison.

The Story of Thomas Cotter
Chapter Five

Early 1995; Thomas Cotter was released from prison. His only visitors during those years had been his old friends Shirley and Bertie. They came down from London once a month to visit and to check his house, in the winter they would turn on the heating to make sure the pipes didn't freeze, in the summer they kept the garden from becoming overgrown and the cobwebs out of the corners of the rooms.

The day he left prison he went home and walked into the house, he didn't take his shoes off, he wiped his feet on the mat then walked on the pristine carpet in his shoes. The smell of carrots and hairspray faintly hit his nostrils.

His car was still in the garage, he wasn't sure if it would start, the battery would be flat but apart from that it should be fine, he had always looked after his cars and serviced them with water, oil check and air at least once a month. Tomorrow he would sort it out.

Tomorrow he would also put the house up for sale, he didn't belong in this part of England.

Tomorrow he would go to London, find a home in Bermondsey. He would return home.

In March 1995 Thomas moved in to a ground floor maisonette flat which had been built a few years before. It was a nice complex, a small cluster of mews-like buildings, twenty flats altogether set around well-kept gardens and old trees. It would allow him his privacy, from what the agent told him these were flats for mainly single people who were out at work each day. A couple had been bought to rent out and the one for sale at the moment had two bedrooms and was easy to keep clean.

Thomas needed two bedrooms for when Barbara was allowed to come and stay with him. As she had got older the visits every other weekend stretched to become once a month and then once every three months. The doctors had told him that since he hadn't been around for the last few years, she had a routine which they didn't really want to disrupt, but perhaps she could come to visit him in a few months' time, once she got used to seeing him again.

He was the only person close to her, the only one left in her life, he couldn't just leave her. He was responsible, she was his daughter. And so he bought the two-bedroomed maisonette.

****

Thomas didn't go out of his way to speak to his neighbours in the Close, he knew two of them by name as they were members of the committee for the management company taking care of the upkeep of the grounds. They introduced themselves and told him that he could knock on their door with any problems he may have.

His routine each day never wavered. On Monday and Friday he would go to the library to return his books and take out new ones. On Thursday he would walk down to The Blue to get his food and groceries for the week. On a Friday, on his way back from the library, he would stop off for fish and chips which he would take home and eat whilst he listened to BBC Radio 4.

He had no specific cleaning day; that was something which had to be done each day, he kept on top of it and there was never even a dirty teaspoon to be found waiting to be washed in the sink. As soon as he finished a cup of tea he would wash the cup and saucer and put it back in the cupboard. He had been trained by the best and the old habits had not deserted him during his years in prison.

The other residents of the Close only knew him as Thomas and that he had moved back to the area where he grew up. He would greet them politely and tip his hat as he passed by. He always wore a shirt and tie and a beige mac which must have once fitted his fuller frame; it now hung from his bony shoulders and down his skinny body.

When he first returned to Bermondsey, Thomas walked to Drummond Road, the way he did all those years ago, the roads had changed and more than once he found himself lost and disorientated by the new buildings. When he got to Drummond road he didn't linger. The time had gone, the factory had closed in 1989 yet, as he got close he could still smell the sweet aroma of biscuits, it lingered in the bricks of every building still standing. It had been the best time of his life and he had allowed it to be taken from him.

After visiting Barbara regularly for a year it was decided that she could visit her father for a few days.

Thomas drove down to the home outside Brighton to collect her. She was silent in the car as they drove back to Bermondsey, her hair was long, thick and wavy, she wouldn't allow anyone to cut it and it was now down to her waist, like the clothes she insisted on wearing it was dyed jet black, with her pale face she looked almost ghostly.

Thomas told her stories of Biscuit Town and how he had played in the streets from morning till night, whether she listened and took in his stories he didn't know, but it was nice talking about those times again.

Barbara didn't sleep well that first night; Thomas had been up most of the night with her. Perhaps it had been a mistake bringing her to the Close, the walls of the flats were thin and noise travels easily. Barbara turned the radio on at two in the morning, full blast and sang along, loudly, with the music. Thomas hated fuss and the thought of disrupting his neighbour's lives. He tried to calm his daughter down, he gave her a tablet which the doctor had given him for her and, eventually, she went back to sleep. Thomas sat in his chair reading his book, waiting for dawn to break through

The next day, Saturday, Thomas asked her what she would like to do.

'Watch television,' she replied with the voice of a petulant teenager.

'I don't have a TV,' Thomas had no need of its entertainment, 'I'll show you the photo albums.' He had many, he had found them in his parent's home when he cleared it out. He had also found a box which his mother had kept, filling it through the years with a babies rattle, his first pair of shoes, drawings and cards he made for her. She had saved so much from his life growing up. He never doubted that he had been loved.

'Photos?' Barbara glared at him, 'where are the photos of my mother? Who are these people you've got plastered everywhere?'

'These are my parents…'

'Where's my mother?'

Thomas stuttered, the truth was, when he was clearing out the house he hadn't kept any photos of his wife. He felt angry with himself, why had he not thought of his daughter? Why did he not save them for her?

'Your mother didn't like her photo taken, she was camera shy.' It was all he could think of to say.

'You're lying, you're a liar. She loved having her photo taken, she posed like Grace Kelly – she told me so.'

'I'm rather hungry, aren't you?' Thomas tried his best to defer the conversation. 'Now, what shall we have for breakfast?' He rose from his chair and went to the kitchen, it was a mess. Barbara must have done it whilst he was in the bathroom getting washed. Cereal had been sprinkled over the worktop, in the sink and on the floor. Bread had been ripped into pieces and thrown around randomly. 'I'll make us some eggy bread shall I?' He cleared the mess as he spoke, 'you like that don't you? With tomato sauce?' he panicked, had he remembered to buy tomato sauce? Life wouldn't be worth living if he'd forgotten it.

'Alright.' Barbara called back, in the flash of a moment she had calmed down, Thomas sighed with relief.

'Right then,' I'll just take this rubbish out to the bin and then we can have our breakfast. Thomas took the bag across the car park to the communal bin, when he returned to his house the front door had been locked.

'Barbara,' he called quietly through the letter box, 'can you please come and open the door.'

'No!' his daughter yelled back, 'this is *my* house and you're not coming in here, ever again!'

Thomas heard the radio blare out, loud pop music, he could feel the pulse in rhythm to the bass. He couldn't see through the front window because of the net curtain so he ran round the back to see if he could see her in the kitchen.

She was in there, pouring oil into the frying pan, visions of the burning pan which his colleague in Brighton had recounted filled his head, he had no idea how to stop her or get her to open the door. He would have to call the home and ask them to help, how they could help, he didn't know, but he couldn't manage this on his own.

It wasn't yet nine o'clock on a Saturday morning, the two committee members would probably still be asleep, which of them was most likely to be up? He chose the one who lived on the other side of the Close, luckily she was awake and up and yes, of course he could use her phone.

Thomas spoke to the doctor at the home who told him that he had no option but to call the police, they would come and help. Thomas was embarrassed and mortified at causing such a scene, when all he wanted was to be insignificant in these people's lives.

The police arrived and broke into his flat, as they swarmed inside Barbara screamed hysterically, she kicked and tried to bite the officers. Thomas watched, he wanted to crumble on the spot, he felt the energy leave his body, he was helpless, he was useless. Yvonne had been right, he was a weak excuse for a man with no back bone.

When the ambulance left, taking Barbara back to Brighton, Thomas made his way across the Close and went to apologise to the committee member for bringing disruption to the community. The woman smiled at him gently and assured him that it was not a problem and she hoped that his daughter would be well enough to return for another visit.

Thomas thanked her knowing that Barbara would never visit him again.

****

Thomas continued to live his life with the routine he had become accustomed to. Both Shirley and Bertie passed away. Apart from the Committee AGM each February their funerals were the only social gatherings he went to.

In 2001, the woman who lived in the flat upstairs from Thomas went to see one of the committee members.

'I'm not sure if I'm worrying over nothing but during the night two days ago there was an almighty crash from Thomas's flat downstairs. The next day I knocked on his door, to make sure he was alright, he didn't answer but I thought nothing of it, he slept at strange times during the day.' She hesitated for a moment wondering if she was creating a mountain out of nothing. 'I've just knocked again and still there's no response, I'm a bit concerned, I've asked around and nobody has seen him, going out to do his errands…at some point I hear either the water running or a door closing, he's a very quiet neighbour at the best of times but at least at some point I can tell he's there…I don't know what I should do.'

'Let me put my shoes on and I'll come over and we'll see if we can get hold of him.' The committee member told her. She had a soft spot for Thomas, he would take in her parcels from the postman when she wasn't home. He was always so polite and when he smiled his whole face beamed with an explosion of creases and wrinkles on his face. She liked the way he would tip his hat whenever he passed her by on the street.

They stood on his step knocking and ringing the doorbell. They tried to peer through the net curtain but they couldn't see a thing. They went round the back to look into the kitchen and the bedroom.

Thomas was on the floor, they could see his feet and legs, the rest of his body was hidden behind a door.

For the second time, the police broke into Thomas's home, only this time it was to discover his dead body.

He had died alone and laid there for such a time, until the extremities of his body had turned black. If it wasn't for his neighbour he would have stayed there, for goodness knows how long.

'Does he have any next of kin?' the police officer asked the neighbour as his colleague called for a doctor to come and proclaim the man dead.

'He has a daughter,' the committee member answered as she looked down at the sad picture of the quiet man of the Close, 'I have his solicitor's details on file…' She looked around the flat, everything was perfectly placed. An old fashioned gilt tea trolley sat by the side of a chair, a rose porcelain tea set stood ready, the trolley was covered in a plastic canopy.

The sideboard with its dainty ornaments had a plastic covering too, so did a vase of faded plastic roses on a side table.

'Maybe he was about to start painting?' The neighbour asked no-one in particular. The policeman looked at her, 'everything is covered in plastic…'

On her way out, the committee member picked up three books from the unused telephone table in the hall. 'I'll take these back to the library for him,' she said quietly, almost to herself, 'I'm sure they know him well, they would like to know.' Before she opened the front door to leave, she ran her fingers over the collar of the raincoat hanging from the peg and smiled, remembering the gentleness of this quiet man. She placed her finger under the rim of the trilby on the peg next to it and tilted the hat slightly, 'good-day Thomas,' she nodded her head and allowed the hat to move back into place, before closing the door behind her.

7. Luca

Three months that summer or *my summer with Lana*?

Luca played with both sentences, whichever way he said them the conclusion came out the same; his world had been filled with an outburst of joy.

Luca spent most of his time travelling; he'd been to every continent on the planet.

He'd faced - and escaped - the unwelcome gestures of remote tribes in Peru.

He'd fled with barely his life intact from drug barons living in the isolated jungle deep inside Thailand's farming communities.

In 2004, after the destructive tsunami, the Indian Government gave authorisation for Luca and a crew of eleven men and women - fellow anthropologists and archaeologists – to set sail around the Andaman Islands in the Indian Ocean to ascertain the level of catastrophic destruction the tsunami had left behind, more specifically; North Sentinel Island. They discovered that the Sentinelese Islanders had survived and were ready to fight; a hail of stones and iron lances assaulted their boat; they were lucky to escape with everyone intact. The Sentinelese were known to either retreat into the deep jungle when ships and boats verged too close to their coral-ringed island, or they would stand on the beach menacingly with arms and armoury raised high, ready to attack, and probably kill, anyone who came too close. Here lives a tribe of peoples who have had no close contact with the outside world and, for them now to have that contact would certainly mean a death sentence through contamination and disease.

Luca himself, originated from Australia. And that was the life he lived.

* * * *

He'd been in Cambridge for less than a week; a visitor on a three month assignment at the Museum of Archaeology and Anthropology. It was his first time in Cambridge and he hadn't yet found his way around, it seemed to be a dizzy place where the streets were placed haphazardly, he had no idea how to get from one destination to the next, but today that wasn't important, today the time was his own.

Luca had been sat on the terrace for two hours, writing notes and reading between top-ups of coffee, water and juice.

He was in no rush to go, or be, anywhere, the tables around him were full. Over the last couple of hours he'd seen the faces on the terrace change several times over. He'd purposely chosen one of the smaller tables; he wasn't in a mood to chat to strangers, no matter how charming they were. Today, he was enjoying the stillness and his solitude in a city heaving with people.

It was nearly lunchtime, Luca felt he should make a move to allow the office crowds a chance to sit in the sunshine, he would have one last cup and then he would go.

****

He didn't see the woman aiming her stride in his direction.

She stood at his table and pointed to the vacant chair. 'Is this chair free…is someone sitting here?' she asked out of politeness.

'No, please…' he replied with the same politeness, as he had done numerous times that morning. Luca stood up and held the back of the chair for her, indicating that she was welcome to take a seat.

The woman thanked him; Luca nodded, smiled and picked up his paper, an excuse not to have to make small talk. He took no offence when the woman moved the chair a few inches further away, she wanted to avoid conversation too.

A young girl came to take the woman's order, Luca interrupted before she left and ordered a final coffee for himself, after this one he would make a move and maybe find a new way back to his apartment through the old backstreets.

He was pleased when he saw the woman take a book out of her bag, it freed him from feelings of obligation to speak to her.

She put her sunglasses on, they hid her eyes and created another barrier between two strangers.

It takes place without thinking doesn't it? Those natural reactions when something happens, someone may trip and drop their shopping – without a second thought you run to help. You see something amusing and you laugh, a little snorting noise, a semi-silent guffaw meant only for yourself.

And so it was when a bike went by, it was pulling at least half a dozen dogs lounging lazily in a brightly painted trailer. The young guy pedalled furiously pulling the weight behind him.

The woman at the table caught a glimpse of the top of a Westie's head - her heart always flipped at the sight of one - she gave her personal chuckling laugh, at the same time as Luca gave his.

Their conversation started from that one moment.
    Luca couldn't remember who spoke first, who said what.
    'I play the cello.' Luca said in response to a question which,

later, he couldn't remember what she had asked.

'I don't know anything about classical music, apart from the obvious one's…Vivaldi...' She told him.

'It's not just the music though,' he smiled, 'it's the story behind the composer which *changes* the music, which makes it real and brings it to life, each piece has a story.'

Her name was Lana, she told him. She didn't live in Cambridge so she had no idea how to get around the quaint back streets either. Lana lived in a village half an hour's drive away.

'I don't have anything on for the rest of the day so, if you're not doing anything would you like to…' Luca stuttered, 'we could go to The Peterhouse Theatre, there's a classical concert on at the college this afternoon,' his voice faltered towards the end of his sentence. 'Sorry,' he apologised at her silent non-response, 'I get rather over enthusiastic about music, I run away with myself a bit…'

'I'd love to go.' Lana said quietly, she was in two minds whether to buy a piece of sculpture from a gallery further up the road, but it would wait for another day.

'You would?' he asked, surprised.

'Yes!' She smiled broadly.

Luca couldn't make out her age, her hair was still dark and her skin was that of a young woman, the signs of maturity manifested when she bent her head forward, showing a slight distortion in the folds of her neck. It didn't matter to him whether she was forty-three; the same age as him or whether she was fifty-eight, all he knew was that he wanted to spend time with her.

Lana was fifty-five and had broken away from a relationship of more years than she cared to count, a relationship with a man who had very nearly broken her soul and left her feeling worthless both as a woman and a human being.

That afternoon was the start of Lana's indoctrination into the world of classics.

Each story Luca told her had her hankering for more.

He told her how, in his deafness, Beethoven chopped the legs off his piano so that he could feel the music beating into his body through the floor - which drove his neighbours downstairs crazy of course. Who was the mysterious lady; his *dearly beloved*? A question which had scuppered and tested the minds of many an academic then, and since.

Mozart; wild and flamboyant who once was engaged as the court musician in Salzburg and died a pauper.

Every spare hour that Luca had he spent it with Lana. They went to London and Luca recited the complete ballad of the Lady of Shallot as they walked along Regent Street after spending the afternoon at The London Coliseum. They'd been to see The Magic Flute, Mozart's fairy tale opera which Luca said was the easiest to get initiated with.

* * * *

Luca told her stories of his life as an anthropologist, travelling to remote places with his work. Lana was enthralled by him and the life he lived.

He told her how there exists a hundred or more groups of people scattered over our planet, tribes who have never had contact with the outside world.

'They have no knowledge of our existence,' he told her, 'all they want is to be left alone, they don't need us and our diseases and they certainly don't deserve to have loggers forcing them off their land and even worse, pointlessly killing them for their land. These tribes,' he told her, 'know nothing outside of their jungle clearing.'

'They must be petrified.' Lana felt deep sorrow for these people.

'They are. They have no notion that anything else exists, can you imagine their terror…?'

'I can't *believe*,' she told him as they ate dinner in a small Italian trattoria in Covent Garden, 'that, by pure chance I meet someone as clever and wonderful as you! All I did was stop for a coffee!' she laughed and shook her head in amazement, 'boy, this spaghetti is good!'

Luca's very presence allowed Lana to slip back to her old self. The person she was before, all those years ago, before Howard had slowly taken her confidence.

Luca was interested in *her*, he wanted to know about the things she liked, the things which got her heart soaring, the loves she'd had and those she had lost.

And so as she told him everything, she felt unleashed. She told him how she had only ever loved one person in her life, but that was long ago.

'Joe, was married,' she said, 'I'm not proud of that fact but I couldn't help it, I tried not to love him…but I did,' she glanced at Luca for his reaction, hoping she wouldn't see a look of distaste curling the corners of his mouth. 'We were young. I couldn't help loving him and, I've never stopped.'

Luca's dark brown eyes shone with depth and warmth, he enveloped her with a strange feeling of security. She had to remind herself that he was *not* Howard, most people were not Howard, Luca wasn't waiting, ready to pour sand on her joy.

'Before all that though,' she leaned across the table with a conspiratorial laugh, 'there'd been a flock of turkeys flapping around in my life…a gigolo, a murdering druggie…and now, there's *you*!' she laughed again, 'what a frigging mixed bag of toys you all are!'

Luca didn't fit in with the world of economics and concrete, he was a gentle, beautiful person, he was probably more suited to a bygone era of flowers in the hair and ban the bomb slogans on t-shirts with flowery flared pants, lazing the day away in a meadow of buttercups and field mice.

Luca had insight and knew Lana better, in those few weeks since they met, than Howard did in all the years they were together.

* * * *

I've booked us into the Langham Hotel in London for a couple of days - Luca pinged the text over to Lana's phone; *are you up for it?* He followed before she had a chance to reply to the first one.

I'm there already, waiting she replied with a smiley face at the end.

Tuesday, early July, the weather was rather overcast but it didn't distract from the gladness Lana felt as she drove to Cambridge and parked at the serviced apartment Luca was renting. They caught the train to London then a cab to The Langham.

'Whoa, look at this shower Luca!' Lana called as she did a tour of their room; he came up behind her and put his arms around her. 'A shower made for two, whaddya think of that?'

she teased as she pressed her body against his.

She sang a ditty which she'd made up; '*Shoo-bop-be-doo let's doo-ka the Lana-Luca*' she sang the words in time to a tune on the radio; Luca threw himself on the bed and laughed aloud as she danced around him, singing her nonsensical song.

Luca couldn't get enough of her; the way her mind worked thrilled him.

'I could never be bored in your company,' he'd told her many times and meant it. Lana's eagerness to learn new things; how she soaked up his words; how she silently listened in sorrow as he told her of the lives of innocent tribes and wild animals which had been shattered by the interference of mankind.

Without words, they were both aware that once Luca's assignment was over, he would be leaving, back to that life which took him to continents far away and beyond civilisation.

Without words they both accepted that. Two different worlds, joining together for a brief moment.

* * * *

They spent the next morning in Covent Garden watching street performers and wandering the shops and indoor markets.

Late morning Luca said he knew just the right place to get a light lunch, Lana happily followed his lead as they made their way toward Charing Cross Road where he hailed a cab, he asked the driver to take them to Wigmore Street, a short walk from their hotel.

He'd planned this over the phone and via emails, he hoped that they had it all set out, ready as he had instructed. He would have liked to go in first, just to make sure, but he would just have to trust that they had done as he asked.

This was the reason why he had brought Lana to London.

'Close your eyes!' Luca held his hand over her eyes and guided her down the street and through a door, 'no peeping! Careful there's a step here…' He led her down a corridor following the concierge who walked silently in front of them until they reached a door, the concierge opened the door and Luca led Lana in.

It was a small room which had a tray of sandwiches, Leonidas chocolates and hot water with herbal tea bags laid out on a table. A comfortable chair sat on one side of the tiny space and a dining chair sat opposite, Lana had no idea what was about to happen.

'I would have ordered champagne but as you don't drink I asked them to substitute it with herby tea bags, I didn't want to risk coffee without a barista in the building!' Luca smiled knowing that they both were rather fussy when it came to how they liked their cappuccino, latte and espresso's. 'I'm just going to go and get something so,' he turned to the small buffet, 'help yourself to a bit of lunch ma'am, and I'll be back shortly.'

Lana laughed at his craziness, she had no idea what he had planned, but, whatever it was she knew it would be special, something thoughtful. No nasty surprises to knock her off her balance and make her feel useless with this man, she shook the thought of Howard and his mean ways from her head.

She took two tea-bags, she liked it strong so that the spices bit her throat, she pressed a button on the flask-like container and hot water trickled out into the mug, she put a few brown bread finger sandwiches onto her plate and sat down on the hard chair. After a few seconds she got up and moved to the easy chair, she put her plate and mug on the small table placed at its side.

Lana didn't know which chair she should be sat in so she stood up again and took a small white, brick of a chocolate, from the box, she ate it in two bites and went back for another as she waited for Luca to come back.

'Sit down,' he said as he came back into the room all excited and big smiles, he put his hands on her shoulders and navigated her to the easy chair as she ate the chocolate she had just put in her mouth, she held another two between her fingers.

'Now, close your eyes again and *do not open* them, not until you hear me say you can.'

Lana did as he asked, she trusted him without question, she put both of the chocolates in the open palm of her left hand, hoping they wouldn't melt, and raised her other hand to cover her eyes, just to make sure she didn't open them with some kind of reflex reaction.

It was less than a minute later when Luca came back into the room, Lana heard thumping and clunking sounds - then came silence.

Silence, before one note quivered through the air, the haunting notes of a cello weeping, it filled the room with such beauty she felt her breath being taken away from her, every hair on her head, her neck, her arms tingled.

Slowly she moved her hand away from her eyes and watched the vision before her, Luca was in another world, his grey and dark streaked hair flopped down over his face as he played the first few notes of Pachelbel Canon, then, out of the speakers in the room came the accompanying sound of a violin, more cellos joined in and more violins filled the air, a flute made its way into the room and together Lana had her own personal orchestra, a magnificent cloud of music to raise her out of a life she had once known, all of this, being led by the finest cello player she ever did see, sitting in front of her very eyes.

She wanted the moment to last forever; she wanted to die in that room with that music carrying her soul to another world.

Luca looked up at her and smiled, she found it very difficult to hold back her tears, it was one of the most beautiful things anyone had ever done for her.

* * * *

'If things had been different, circumstances…' Luca looked across the table. It was their last dinner together; tomorrow he would fly back to Australia. His eyes were smiling as he looked at her.

'*You*,' she leaned across the table, 'have given me the most wonderful summer I have known in years and you're right, if circumstances were different, I would be on the next plane, following you to Oz.' She smiled at his smile.

'It's been good, hasn't it?'

'It's been the best.' She said truthfully. In a matter of weeks Luca had, effortlessly, revived the characteristics and confidence which had been snoozing in her marrow, he brought her back to that comfort zone where she came face-to-face with her old self again. In just a few short weeks Luca had annihilated the inadequacy, that which her life during the previous years with Howard had slowly ingrained in to her spirit. 'I've never known anyone as gifted and lovely as you,' Lana told him honestly.

'I absolutely *adore* you, I've cherished every moment I've spent with you.' Luca pressed his lips against the back of her hand, 'I love the way you gobble up knowledge, how you're are always hungry to learn more, how you come close to tears when you hear something beautiful, whether it's music, words or a lonely bird singing. *Aw*,' he sighed, 'how you laugh out loud, sometimes, it's a *very dirty* laugh, yet other times it is full of joy and fun.'

'I love your passion for music and your knowledge. Wow, you have no idea how I could sit and listen to you for hours and days, you've seen and experienced *so* much, yet you are so humble with all your knowledge. You've no idea what it has meant to me, you sharing those stories with me.'

'Ah! I love these self-appreciation conversations that we indulge ourselves in, they nourish the ego!' Luca's laugh rang out.

'Well, another thing,' Lana smiled light-heartedly, 'how you always keep a few pound coins in your pocket,' she saw Luca pull a face at her words. 'Aha!' she chortled, 'every time we walked past a homeless person busking in the street or stood with his hand open, *I saw you*, you'd slip money into his hand or flip it into his hat!' Lana made the motion with her hand secretly sliding into her thigh pocket and flipping coins on the ground, '*Purrphwat*' she clicked her tongue.

'Oh well, if we're getting on to that sort of behaviour, *you* went one further, *so I heard…*'

'Nah?' she sniggered in a strange way, 'what did you hear?' Lana didn't know what he meant, but it still made her laugh.

'That busker who sits near John Lewis-'

'Oh no!' she covered her face with her hands in embarrassment before regaining her composure, 'oh well, anyway, he's another one you regularly flip a coin at!'

'Yep! He told me that you went up to him with a bag and, in that bag you'd put a few tins of dog food and biscuit treats for his mutt and some Frontline for his fleas.'

'The poor animal always scratches! A bit o' frontline on the neck, that's all he needed. Maybe the old boy should have used a drop or two on himself.' They snickered and chortled as they talked.

'Oh, yeah, by the way, he sold the tins of dog food.'

'What? No!' her laughter stopped.

'He had to, because he had no sodding way to open the tins.'

Her laughter burbled over his words.

'Look what you've done to me!' she told him as their

laughter finally subsided. 'A chance meeting and you've eliminated all the shitty dross it took Howard *years* to build up in me. Tsk, he would be *so pissed off* with you destroying all his hard work.'

It may have been her fault, she had often thought, you know how some people bring out the bad part of you? The not so good side, how they irritate you for no reason on earth and make you feel angry and annoyed?

She could have been that person in Howard's life, the one who released the brute inside of him which he then took out on her. Maybe, in some obscure way, it *had* been her fault after all.

'I still can't get my head around it, how anyone could treat you in such a way? If you were mine…well, not mine because we don't own people, but you know what I mean, if you were mine then I would want to make very single hour of every day special, to share it with you. I would take you to Milan and Naples, we would see *Nabucco* and *Madama Butterfly*, then fly off to India where the elephants roam freely along the beach. I would sit quietly under a tree and watch them, and I would watch you, you doing your yoga.'

Lana wanted to write his words down, have him dictate them into her new hi-tech smart phone, there to listen when she didn't feel as strong as she did at that moment, when he was by her side.

'And if you were mine,' she replied in the same tone, 'being with you every day would be special enough for me.'

These were not the seriously cheesy words of lovers blinded by a romantic liaison, it was truthful, frolicsome banter between two friends, transient lovers who would go their own way, each one fulfilled differently by their encounter.

'That's the summer gone then,' Luca whistled as they walked out of the restaurant, 'soon, your favourite season will be here,' he looked down and smiled at her, he opened his arm inviting her to put hers through his before they set off walking back to his apartment.

'I can take you to the airport tomorrow,' she said.

'No, I've got a car coming to pick me up, it's probably better that way.'

'Yes, you're right,' she answered thoughtfully. 'Luca?'

'Hmm?' he bent and rested his cheek against her head.

'Will you recite the Lady of Shallot again for me?'

Ten minutes later they arrived at his apartment, just as he spoke the last line of the epic ballad.

They made their way up to his apartment in silence whilst holding on to each other, each one had their own thoughts.

* * * *

When Luca got up the next morning to go to the bathroom Lana placed a small box on his pillow which she had swathed with colourful ribbons, inside sat a small four-inch cello inside a water-tight Perspex case which had been moulded and shaped to fit the miniature replica. The cello had been hand-carved from a piece of maple; the fingerboard, tailpiece and pegs were made of ebony, and the four strings were titanium, it was a small perfect replica complete with its own matching bow.

Lana had called antique dealers, old contacts from her days with Howard. One of them had sourced this perfect specimen for her.

'What's this?' Luca jumped on to the bed, he touched the Perspex covering.

'It's only something small, to keep with you when you come upon *uncontacted tribes*, you can charm them with your music.' She touched his fingers as she spoke and showed him how to open the Perspex case to reveal the perfectly formed cello and bow.

'Whoa, this is amazing,' he said slowly as he carefully held the instrument. He moved the bow over the strings to produce a small tinny note. 'I love it!' He said quietly as he closed the seal of Perspex back around it. 'You, are bloody amazing!' he jumped on top of her and made her squeal with laughter.

Luca had been sent to her on a brief expedition, her guiding spirits had brought him to her to show her the old world she knew and the goodness of people in it, to lift her back into that place where she should be and revive her heart and soul, and ready for her life, which was, unknowingly to her, waiting round the corner.

'Those buskers will miss you,' she told him thoughtfully. 'And I will too.'

* * * *

Luca watched the tarmac speed by, the plane rose into the sky, in his melancholy he felt a solace settle inside of him. He was used to unexpected adventures jumping out to grab him unawares; surprising him with their intensity, but meeting Lana had been a different, though a no-less remarkable, experience. He'd been living in a world which excluded the twenty-first century, cutting himself off from the present time, he felt more comfortable and at ease in a world without the consumerism, where nature thrives and the smells of the jungle, mingling with murky rivers, were the first things to catch hold of his senses each morning when he awoke.

And then she had come along, out of nowhere, making him laugh and filling him with fascination, she briefly brought him back to the world he was born in to and he loved her for that but now, it was time for him to return to that sphere he was truly at home in; remoteness, sounds echoing and rustling through the jungle, the rolling ocean and a mass of stars overhead.

* * * *

Lana put the suitcase on her bed. She felt a bit of an emptiness swimming inside of her but, it came hand in hand with the anticipation of something exciting. Three months had turned back time, she was back to her old self, she was ready to move on with life.

She opened the suitcase; a CD sat on top, a recording of the concert he played, just for her. She read the small card Luca had written; *I don't think that I can ever forget you.*

Lana smiled as the first few notes of the cello, Pachelbel Canon, filled her small cottage. The future, to her, was unknown but fate was already working and it had begun by bringing her back to her old self, in preparation for what was to come.

This short story is an off-shoot in cahoots with
The Biggest Lie
and
Truth Unscrewed
by
Lisbeth Foye
"Luca" has previously been available as a free download from Smashwords and Goodreads

Made in the USA
Charleston, SC
26 February 2015